Advance Praise

"*The Ballad of Huck & Miguel* breathes new life into Mark Twain's most enduring and iconic character, setting the inimitable and indomitable Huck Finn loose in modern Los Angeles on an adventure every bit as thrilling, provocative, humane, and laugh-out-loud funny as the original. DeRoche channels Twain's winking, laconic prose with effortless aplomb, but it's what's new about this timeless tale that makes it such an urgent and worthwhile read. DeRoche imagines the Los Angeles River as a dark, magical underworld inhabited by all sorts of extraordinary beasts and characters—a place where anything can happen.

"Above all this is a story about America through the eyes of an outsider and an immigrant. In short, through the eyes of those Real Americans too often and too easily overlooked. The text is illustrated with linocuts by Daniel González, who finds beauty and hope in the darkest, dingiest corners of the American dream. Together, DeRoche and González have crafted a tour de force that captures the feral, beating heart of a mythical Los Angeles where Twain himself would certainly have felt at home."

— MAX BORENSTEIN,
screenwriter of *Kong: Skull Island* and *Godzilla*

"A bully tale! *The Ballad of Huck & Miguel* channels the timeless voice of Huckleberry Finn to tell an engrossing and amusing adventure story for our times. It is an homage worthy of its inspiration, and I am sure Mark Twain himself would be right proud of the way DeRoche has modernized and maybe here and there even improved upon his original. DeRoche keeps what is best and most enduring about Huckleberry Finn—the timeless, unpretentious wisdom and un-miseducated insight—and brings it to bear on our contemporary pretensions and delusions, and tells a great and touching story, too."

— DAN GREANEY, writer for *The Simpsons* and *The Office*

"A thrilling reboot of a classic that, on the surface, is a magical urban adventure. But it's also a clever exploration of the immigrant experience in America. The ballad awashes us with our past, our future, and a cogent understanding that, on the great river of life, there are many barriers, but no real borders."

— GLORIA ROMERO,
former Majority Leader of the California State Senate

"More than 130 years ago, Mark Twain set Huckleberry Finn on a journey down the Mississippi River and deep into the American consciousness. It has been argued that the journey will never be over, since we'll continue to be challenged by this story on so many profound levels as individuals and a nation. Captivating and compelling proof of this can be found in each chapter of *The Ballad of Huck & Miguel*, Tim DeRoche's bold reimagining of Twain's novel. DeRoche daringly transports Twain's characters, themes, plot elements, and narrative voice to modern-day Los Angeles, managing to make this ongoing journey seem at the same time fresh and familiar—and, of course, incredibly relevant."

— MARK DAWIDZIAK, Mark Twain scholar and
editor of *Mark My Words: Mark Twain on Writing*

"Daniel González's lovingly detailed linocut illustrations mark not only Huck and Miguel's vivid journey along the L.A. River, but also draw focus on a world where the lines in life—rivers, borders, boundaries in the street—remain freshly cut by ancient ghosts. González works within the wonderful tradition of printmaking that has produced some of the greatest artists of Mexico and the US. His work captures the beauties and dangers of a California that perpetually cradles the newcomer."

— DANIEL HERNANDEZ,
former Mexico City bureau chief for VICE

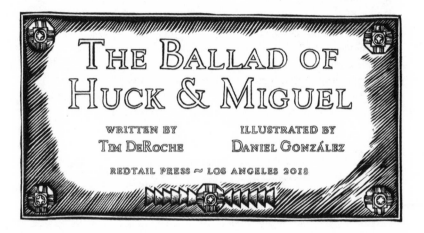

THE BALLAD OF HUCK & MIGUEL

WRITTEN BY
TIM DEROCHE

ILLUSTRATED BY
DANIEL GONZÁLEZ

REDTAIL PRESS ~ LOS ANGELES 2018

REDTAIL PRESS

This is a work of fiction. All incidents and dialogue, and all
names and characters, are products of the author's imagination
and are not to be construed as real. Other than obviously factual
locations, all places are also products of the author's imagination and
are not to be construed as real.

Published by Redtail Press
Los Angeles, California
www.redtailpress.com

**RAYMOND
·PRESS·**

Produced for Redtail Press by
Raymond Press
Altadena, California
www.prospectparkbooks.com

**Library of Congress Cataloging-in-Publication Data in
progress**
DeRoche, Tim
ISBN 978-0-9992776-7-6 (hardcover)
Fiction

Book layout and design by Amy Inouye, Future Studio
Printed in the United States of America

CONTENTS

Notice

Nothwithstanding the primitive literary practices of the nineteenth century, persons who read this narrative will not be subject to prosecution, banishment, or hostile gunfire. I can, however, make no such assurances to those who should decline to read it.

THE AUTHOR

Me and Pap Light Out
for California

YOU don't know about me without you've been to St.
Petersburg which is in Missouri, which is where everything
starts. That's a beautiful place right up on the big river. It's
a wild place too, where there's all sorts of bully critters in
the woods, and some of the people are just as wild as the
critters. But there's some regular folk too. Nuthin don't
change in St. Petersburg but real slow. My friend Ben
Rogers, his mama says that time done forgot us altogether
and that the people are talking and living just like it's still
the eighteen hunderts, even though everybody knows we
already passed two thousand year. Well, I can't vouch for it.
She might be stretching it a little bit, but then again maybe
not. It warn't a good thing but a bad thing, in her view,
for folks to get stuck like that. As for me, I like a place that
don't change too much. There's other places—I'll tell you
'bout one of 'em—where things change all the time so fast

that a body can't barely keep up. And I come to see the profit in that, too.

This here is the full true story of how I left St. Petersburg for California and went on the run from the 'thorities with a real live illegal Mexigrant. And I even got rid of my Pap for good. Me and Miguel, we had a right bully 'venture on that concrete river in Los Angeles, which might be the biggest city that ever was. I'll tell it to the best of my 'bilities. There might be a few stretchers along the way, but I'll work 'em in nice and proper, so as you won't notice too much.

So I'm just gonna tell it. For near on two months, Pap had been going on about California. He got to thinking that his troubles was all the 'sponsiblity of Missouri and St. Petersburg and the lowdown people who lived there. "Sometimes I've a mighty notion to leave this place once and for good," he says to me. "Alfonse he says that a man of quality has more of a chance in California. That's a place where nobody's gonna hold a man down, like they do here." Alfonse was his friend in a way, though I warn't too keen to have a friend like that myself. Pap said in Los Angeles a man could get rich just by walking down the street and picking up all the money that the other folks dropped while they warn't paying tension. He said there was great big palm trees as tall as a mountain and an ocean so vast that it would make the big river seem like a muddy little creek running through the forest. "That's the place for you and me, Huck. We can do better in a place like that." And he said that the women there was of a higher quality than in Missouri and that they had discerniminating tastes.

"They knows a real man when they sees one, Huck. Not like these ones here." At first he said that we might could take an aeroplane out to California, which was bully by me, but then later on he started talking like he wanted to drive his old camper all the way acrossed the country, so as we'd have a place to sleep when we got there.

Well I turned it over in my brain and had a good long think about it. Supposing that California was such a bully place, it might make for a powerful good change. But Pap—I was pretty uncomfortable about being alone with him for a good long while. Every now and again he'd get hisself cleaned up and sober and he'd make to get a job for a time. But that warn't for long. Pretty soon he'd find hisself lickered up all over again and get handy with his ol' leather belt, and he warn't too kind to me in times like that.

So I reckoned that I wouldn't go to California with Pap and I'd try to get away from him and maybe he'd leave without me and I could get free of him that way. I run off with Ben Rogers to the woods, and we fashioneered a lean-to where I could sleep under and made a hole in the ground where we hid a pot full of food with a rock on top of it to keep out the critters. Every night Ben would go back to his house to sleep and then in the morning—on the way to school—he'd stop by to say hullo and drop off such truck as he'd been able to borrow. There was corn-bread and a couple of green apples that was pretty sour but good sour and some cheese that had gone hard and crispy around the edges but I didn't mind. One time he even brung a piece of cherry pie that was just about the best thing I ever had. I shared Ben a bite or two even though he said that he'd most made hisself sick the night before by eating two and a half pieces after his supper. Ben wanted to stay there with me too, but I told him he warn't old enough, seeing how he had just turned seven. I was almost nine years old, if you believed what my Pap said, which is the proper age for living wild out in the woods.

At night I'd lay under the lean-to and look out the open end up at the sky and watch all the stars turn through the black like they was on a giant wheel. I thought about all the folks out in California and I got to wondering if they seen the same stars as me or whether they might see different ones altogether. Or maybe they might not see stars at all but just diamonds in the sky hanging still from silk threads. Maybe that's why they was so rich out there. Every time they run out of money they could just reach up and pick a diamond star, just like they was picking an apple off a tree. I knowed I was just dreaming up magical things, but it was a nice and beautiful thought and I hoped that there might be someplace where it was true, even if it warn't California.

I didn't have much in the way of possessions. Just that old pot buried in the ground and a pair of old shoes that I could use in the river, so as not to get my regular shoes wet and muddy. Oh, and of course I had my blade with me all the time. Pap had told me to get rid of it, but I warn't inclined to do that, seeing as it was the only thing that I had from my mama. He had a prejudice against her on account of her leaving him for being a lowdown dirty drunk. It warn't really a proper knife—Ben Rogers's mama told me that it was the type of blade that was used

to open up letters from people who live far away. But it was solid enough, and I reckoned that I could use it to fend off any bandits who might stumble acrossed my little lean-to. I thought I'd try to catch and kill a pheasant with it, but I couldn't never get near enough to kill one. I had more luck down at the river. I catched a couple crawfish and then used my blade like a spit to cook 'em up till they was all meaty on the inside. But there warn't enough to 'em. You'd have to catch two dozen just to have one good meal. It was better to have a proper boil like we did last summer and just boil up hunderts of 'em all at one time, so everybody'd have enough. But I didn't have an idea about how a body would catch so many of 'em all at once.

It got so I could sleep pretty good even with sticks and stones sticking into my back and critters a-crawling on my arms and noises in the night. After a couple nights it seemed most normal. I reckon most anything might come normal if a body got used to it and didn't have no choice. Well I did have a choice and I got to like that little lean-to in the woods. It got to be so I most forgot about Pap and all his troubles. I knowed he warn't far away—and prob'ly looking for me if he hadn't given up and lit out for California—but that didn't matter 'cause it seemed like I was all alone in the world, 'cept for the critters in the woods and Ben Rogers my friend who come to bring me food.

One morning Ben come early and said that he had a surprise for me and wanted me to come into town with him. Well at first I relucted because I knowed that Pap could be around town and—even if he warn't—then somebody wouldn't be none to happy about me running around in the woods like a savage and would most like to get a-holt of me and sivilize me and put me back in school, which warn't a comfortable idea for me.

But Ben was powerful persuasive. He said there was something for to see and that maybe I might come out of it with some bully loot that would make my little lean-to more like the cargo room of a pirate ship with treasure and weapons and such truck as they stole from regular decent folk. Well that got me excited 'bout the possibilities and so I followed Ben into town all the while looking hither and forth for Pap. I hoped that he was gone for California already or maybe blind drunk, so he wouldn't even notice me if I stepped over his own body on the ground.

Ben took me right out to old Mrs. Loftus's general store. Around back was a monstrous big trash bin. Ben climbed right in and—being a good friend and a trusting one—I followed him up and over. Well Ben was right. It was just about the biggest corn-o-copious trash bin you ever did see. There was trinkets and gadgets and breaked dishes that you could use for a dagger and even an old wooden mop that would serve for a saber in a pinch. Ben said that Mrs. Loftus was doing her annual inventory and that meant she had to get rid of all the stuff that was breaked or returned or stuff that nobody wanted no more.

"You know what they say about Mrs. Loftus?" Ben he asked me.

"That she's a witch?" Tommy Barnes had sweared that he seen her out in the woods building a fire to cook up a stew of little babies. That's what witches do when they're hungry.

"I'll bet some of this stuff is enchanted like."

I didn't give too much truck to such talk. But it never does a body good to disregard the more fantastical possibilities. If she warn't a witch, then there wouldn't be no harm in giving her the wide berth that a witch would deserve. And if she was a witch, then such a notion might just save your life one day.

I bent down and picked up an old alarm clock from the bottom of the bin. I couldn't tell whether it was still a-keeping time. But it was a bully find no matter what. I got a little tingly feeling when I held it up close to my eyes.

"Hey look, Ben. Look what I found."

But he warn't paying no tension to me. He was looking over the edge of the trash bin at the back door of the store, like he was spooked or something. Pretty soon the door opened up, and his eyes went all wild and big, like a cat backed into the corner of a barn or a coon catched in a leg trap.

"WITCH!" Ben Rogers practically yelled my ears out. I could see that it was old Mrs. Loftus with an old straw broom. It looked like she was just sweeping out the back hall, but Ben he looked like she was trying to turn him into a toad or something like. And when she heard him scream, she screamed right back. And she come after us with the broom a-waving in the air.

"You get out of here, you rapscallions!"

This time it was Ben following me. I fell when I jumped out of the bin and scrapped up my knee pretty good. But before you knowed it, I was running with Ben not far behind, from the sound of his footprints. I looked down and I was pretty satisfied with myself to realize that I hadn't dropped the alarm clock. It was still in my hand.

"And don't you come back here no more!"

She was still yelling but it was further away now. She warn't chasing us. So we was good as free.

At the edge of the building, I rounded the corner, feeling pretty good about how things turned out, 'cept we left behind a lot of good loot. But I warn't watching where I was running and I slammed right into a pair of thick black boots that seemed as solid as a wall made from brickabrack. Of course it was my Pap. And he warn't none too happy.

CHAPTER 2

I Most Get Shot by
a Man with a Donkeytail

NEXT thing I re-
member I was waking
up from a long, long
sleep. My head was all
fuzzy like, and I didn't
know what day it was.
I figgered right away
that Pap had whacked
me good for trying to
get loose of him. He'd
done it before, and it
was times like that when
you warn't sure if you'd
slept for just a couple
minutes or for well nigh
a week. Sometimes you

wouldn't even know where you was at. This time, though, I knowed right away. It was Pap's camper. And I was up above in the space above the driver's seat. That's where Pap let me sleep when I was with him. It was a bully camper with all sorts of snaky pipes and secret compartments and other such stuff as boys like me love, and I liked it well enough 'cept for the body that lived there.

I pulled back the curtain and looked down below. There was Pap, laid out on the floor with a bottle right near him, most like he dropped it when he fell. He was a-snoring and a little puddle of saliver had collected under the corner of his mouth. He warn't too ornery in this condition.

So I let the curtain fall back closed, and I pretended that he warn't there at all. First thing I seen was that old alarm clock still firm in my hand. And I was good and satisfied that I'd managed to hang onto it. I held it up and 'xamined it good. It warn't ticking no more, but that didn't mean it warn't no good. I pulled out my blade from the inside of my sock, where I kept it stowed when I warn't using it, and I started a-pryin' at the front of the clock. My blade was pretty good for a job like that, and pretty soon I'd got the cover off. Then I was able to turn the hands any which way I wanted to. First I went backward and thought about the past and everything that had happened to me and my Pap and how there was lots of good stuff mixed in with the bad. I couldn't see no profit in thinking about all the bad stuff, so I tried real hard to think on the good stuff, like the time my Pap took me out and learned me how to shoot a squirrel out of a tree. Or the time that

Ben Rogers and me found an old butt that had only been smoked about halfway through, and so we each got about three good puffs in before it went out.

And then I got to turning the hands the other way and thinking about what come next, the future as they call it. I kept turning and turning the clock hand and I hoped that maybe it was enchanted and it would give me a vision of what was to happen to me. But nuthin come, no visions at all. So finally I reckoned that the future might be most like the past with the good and the bad all mixed together. That's prob'ly how it is for mos' folks and prob'ly how it'd be for me. That's okay, I thought.

Pretty soon I turned the clock over and started a-pr-yin' at the back. It was tougher to get that part off, but I'm pretty handy with my blade and I made a job of it at last. It snapped open like a clam from the bottom of the river once you got your blade inside the mouth part. Inside the clock was all sorts of gears and gadgets and other magical things. There was a little silver bell in there too. I couldn't help myself but flick it with my finger. "TINGGGGG!" it goes real loud and clear and, well, that kinda breaked the spell because then I heard a grunt somewheres down below. Uh-oh, I thinks to myself. I done it. I waked up Pap.

I pulled back the curtain and looked down. But it turns out the little bell hadn't woken him up after all, just maybe stirred him a little bit. Seeing that this might be my best chance to get free again, I swung down from up above and used the front seat as a foothold to climb down to the floor. I stepped over him nice and quiet, but he prob'ly wouldn'ta noticed if I'd have stomped right down on his head.

I opened and closed the door nice and gentle, just to be safe. And then I had to squint. The sun was powerful bright. It was like the day after a snowstorm when the sun come up a-blazing and all that snow is shining bright so as to blind a body who tries to open his eyes. But there warn't no snow here. Just white sand. I reckoned that we must have made it to California already, 'cause there was mountains out yonder, and they warn't like the green hills back home but instead was bare and rocky and glinty in the sun. I must have lost a couple days at least.

Well there ain't no use in mourning for lost days when you got a perfectly good one right in front of you. This was my chance for a real 'venture so I started walking toward those mountains. I stopped to uricate and decided that I could do a good turn so did it right on top of a little flower that looked like it needed a drink real bad. Pretty soon I come to strangest lake you ever did see. It was flat

and still, most dead like. And it smelled worse than a skunk that's been laying in the road for near on two week. On the shore there was piles and piles of dead fish, rotting in the sun. The bulk of them warn't even fish no more but just skeletons. I took out my blade and slid it right through the eye of one of them fish skeletons and picked it up so I could look at it up close and personable. It was one of the most bully things I ever saw and one of the most ugly too. It seemed like he was looking at me through his empty eye hole, asking me why I come here to disturb the peace and quiet. Well I didn't like that line of questioneering, so I threw him back down on the ground with his friends.

It was alright too, because just then I spotted an old building not too far off from the lake. It was an old motel that was boarded up with old wood. When I got up close, I could see through the cracks in the wood of one of the rooms, and it looked like it must have been real fancy afore it got closed up. I'll bet those rich California people liked it a lot. I found an old sign that said "Salton Sea Resort" and so I reckoned that's where I was, the Salton Sea. And I wondered what had happened there. Maybe there was a war or something and all the rich people had been drived off to higher land.

The swimming pool was all empty, 'cept for a nice old comfy chair. I jumped down in there and pushed the little lever so the chair would lay back more like a bed. I was suddenly mighty comfortable and I looked up at the sky and watched the clouds. They moved fast, and I wondered if maybe these clouds hadn't come from Missouri just like us. Maybe they was headed to Los Angeles too. Maybe they was aiming to be richer clouds than they was now. Or maybe they didn't have no concerns and was just a-blow-ing with the wind wherever they did go.

I think I fell asleep in that chair, 'cause before I knowed

it the sun was further up in the sky and it warn't none too comfortable to be laying right under it. So I got to exploring around the sea—at least, that's what they called it, but to my eyes it was more of a lake. A body of water can't rightly claim to be a sea without which it's got pirates and whales and giant squid—at least that's how we was learned in Missouri. But all around the lake was the strangest sights you ever did see. It most gave me the fantods. There was dead trees, some of 'em sticking up out of the water. And there was dead birds a-laying everywhere, 'cept not in big piles like the fishes. There was a monstrous bully bus that was sinking into the ground and had prob'ly been there a hundert years or maybe more. There was some more buildings, and all over the walls was the ignorantest kind of words and pictures made with paint, the kind that come from a squirt can. Some of the pictures was pretty and some of 'em was pretty plain, like something a child would make with a crayon. I couldn't make it out. But all around there was also huge birds—living birds—acting as if all of this was just as normal as could be. There was pelicans and skinny white birds that most looked like an alien. And I even saw a little owl that come out of a hole in the ground, instead of flying down from a tree like a proper owl.

Well I wandered further and further going from one awful sight to the next. California sure was strange and beautiful and warn't at all like I 'magined it. Pretty soon I come up on a shack surrounded by a bunch of ghostful-looking trees that most made me shiver. There was music playing from the shack so I reckoned that some-

body was prob'ly home and I snuck up real slow like a cat
on the lookout for its supper.

As I come up closer, there was something there that
really got my tension. It was an old truck most like something that you would see in a museum, 'cept it was right
out in the open. Well I couldn't help but run out and look
at it up close. Inside was a couple of old beer bottles and
a snakeskin bigger than any one I'd ever seen before and
right away I knowed it was a rattlesnake, because of the
shaker on the end. The window was open just a crack,
but I thought maybe I could get my hand through there
to take a closer look. I warn't meaning to steal it or even
borrow it but just look at it up close and compare it to the
memories of the snakeskins from back home.

But my hand warn't even all the way through when
I heard a little tinkle from behind me. Well I just about
jumped out of my hide and spun around. There was a man
there, on the porch. He was old and wrinkled up with skin
brown like a grocery bag. His hair was long and white and
pulled back in a donkeytail like a girl. But he warn't no girl.

I decided to make friendly like.

"Hey there, mister. This your truck?"

He didn't answer, and now I noticed that he was leaning on a shotgun most like it was a cane or a crutch.

"She sure is bully," I told him. That's usually a good
way to make folks feel good. You tell 'em something nice
about theyselves or about something that belongs to them.

But he still didn't make to answer. I was beginning to
think maybe he was deaf or dumb or such like. But then
he shifted his weight a little bit, and he picks up the shot-

gun and next I know he's pointing the gun right at me, most like he wants to shoot me. I couldn't hardly move. He had a wild look in his eye, like a dog that got the rabies. My heart jumped up and tried its best to get outta there on its own.

Well I turned and run. It ain't my normal policy to flee from trouble but I reckoned that I didn't have much choice in the matter. The man had a gun and I didn't. It warn't a fair match. And I didn't mean him no harm anyways. I couldn't see him no more, but I heard a laugh-cackle. I couldn't help but turn around and peek back. The old man was laughing most like a hyena. Then he looked down the gun again, but serious this time, and I knowed he was like to shoot this time, so I run even harder.

CRACK!

I heard the gunshot and I fell and my face slammed right down into the sand. For a minute, I was sure that I was shot through and that I was just as good as dead. But my body knowed better than my brain that I warn't shot and just fell. So my body got itself up and started running again even afore my brain figgered out that I didn't have no holes in me yet.

I run and run until I couldn't hardly run no more, even after I couldn't hear him laughcackle no more.

CHAPTER 3

Pap Learns Me Not to Sociate with Mexigrants

AFTER a while I found a road that seemed to aim me back toward the camper. I warn't eager to get back to Pap, but I reckoned that I would ride with him out to Los Angeles and then maybe I could get away from him. If I got free from him here, I wouldn't stand much chance, without I learned myself how to kill and eat a pelican or a ground owl. And even then it seemed that maybe the people out here had rabies or at least some good portion of them. It could be dreadful lonesome to live in a place like that.

So I walked the road, right down the middle, following the yellow paint. And I found a rock that I could kick along, so as to pass the time and to forget about the old man who wanted to kill me. I had my head down and focused real hard on kicking that rock just right, so I was surprised when I heard a voice.

"Hey kid! Could you give me a hand here?"

It was an illegal Mexigrant. Only he was talking like a regular man from California. Pap had warned me that—despite all the 'vantages that California had—we'd have to be careful 'cause the whole place was swarming with illegal Mexigrants. There warn't too many at home, though Pap worked at a factory for a while—before he got hisself fired—and he said that they was a-starting to take jobs in the factory. Pap said that they was of a lower stock than us. They was prone to do what they was told by the bosses and work hard, and he said that jus' showed that they was devious and out to get regular folk like me and him, that sooner or later they'd take all the jobs and become the bosses and then we'd be like aliens in a country that was rightly ours. I reckoned that the way to become a boss was to put away the bottle and not show up for work blind drunk, but Pap had a different way of thinking.

This particular Mexigrant was trying to put up a tent—and not making too good of a job of it. You see, it was really a two-man job, but I seen his wife over yonder making something on the grill. Something that smelled powerful pleasing. So I hurried over to help the man all the while thinking about how this might enable me to fernagle some victuals for to eat.

Most like he read my brain, he says, "My wife is making breakfast. You like carnitas?"

"Sure," I says even though I hadn't never heard of them before. "No problem, mister."

He smiled at me, not like a typical Mexigrant at all. And we managed to spring that tent up in the air in no time at all. It made a mighty satisfying *thwup* sound when it come up. He handed me some metal spikes and we both went 'round the edges of the tent making sure that it was nice and secure in the desert sand. When I stood up, I noticed he was looking me over, like I was bug in a jar or such like.

"Where you from, kid?"

"St. Petersburg. Missouri."

"That's a long way off, huh?"

"My pap and me drove all the way acrossed these United States. Come to California to seek our fortunes." I reckoned he didn't need to know about all my troubles with my Pap.

"Well, I wish you luck. You certainly wouldn't be the first."

By now his wife was entering the picture. "Who's ready for some tacos?" She was smiling so big and true it most breaked my heart. I reckoned that I wouldn't mind being an illegal Mexigrant if someone as beautiful as that was my mama. And the carnitas, as they called them, was steaming on the plate and smelled so good I could barely stand it. But the Mexigrant, he decided that the social niceties was more important than a body's nutritional acquirements.

"Honey, this is Mr.——. I didn't get your name."

"I'm Huckleberry. Huckleberry Finn. Mos' folks just call me Huck." And I didn't waste no time saying it neither.

"Nice to meet you Huck. Help yourself to a taco. You've earned it."

She reached out with the plate so that I could see all that warm sticky meat that was wrapped in some sort of flat yellow bread. I didn't hardly know how to pick it up. "Here take this one," she says. "It's the biggest." And she handed it to me. It was just as good as it looked, even better. And before I knowed what happened it was gone into my mouth and I had grabbed another. While I was chewing, I heard the lady whisper to her husband. She says, "He's *hungry*." And she was right.

Now Pap had a way of disterrupting even the smallest bit of peace and goodness that you might find in this life. And that's what happened this time too. I was just in the midst of enjoying that second taco when I heard a voice in the distance, and you could tell that the voice warn't right.

"HUCKLEBERRY FINN!"

I turned to look and saw the camper not too far off. I must have come further back than I thought. That's what happens when you kick a rock for a while. You lose track of time and geogerphy.

But I didn't have time for thoughts like that just then. I was just afeard.

"THERE AIN'T NO USE IN HIDIN', YOU SLIMY LITTLE TOAD!"

I coulda run off or tried to hide in the tent. But I reckoned that it warn't my time to be free of Pap just yet. And so I went back to the camper. I can't remember if I said goodbye or thank you to the Mexigrants.

Now Pap was a lot smarter than you'd think, especially when he waked up and hadn't gotten back on the bottle yet. He knowed right away where I'd been and warn't none to happy about it. As I come up, he grabbed me by the shirt and dragged me back inside. I pulled free of him for a second, and he chased me 'round and 'round. But finally he got holt of me and smushed my face down into the little table where we ate. I knowed I was in for a whupping when I heard his belt slide through the loops like a copperhead a-slithering through the branches of a tree.

"You will not—," he says with his hand high in the air, and then he brung that belt down on my backside. It made a terrible THWAP sound but it was a couple seconds before I felt the sting. And then he finally got around to finishing his sentence.

"—take charity from those people! Ain't what I give you good enough?"

Another thwap. I ain't a-gonna let him see me cry,

I thinks to myself.

"What would your mama say if she was alive? She wouldn't say nuthin. She'd only jus' cry to see what her son's become."

There was another thwap. And it hurt me good enough, I suppose. But what stung me the most was that last thing that Pap said. But I kept my cryin' on the inside and didn't let him see it.

Well it warn't too long till Pap had us on the road again. And he was a-yelling and a-cussing as he was wont to do when he got hisself all worked up.

"Oh, yes. This is a wonderful gov'ment. They leave the doors wide open. C'mon in! And then they acks all surprised when all these grasshoppers take over the country."

I was up above, trying to protect my backside from all the bumps, but I could hear him clean and clear even after

I put a pillow over my head.

"These illegal Mexigrants ain't got no truck with the law. They got no problem taking a man's money, his food, his job. Why, I was a-gonna stop drinkin' and maybe go back down to the plant, but then Alfonse, he tells me, well, they hired a Mexigrant in your place. And I thinks to myself, what kind of man would I be if I allowed myself to go beggin' back for my job from a man who would hire an illegal Mexigrant. It ain't right, Huck. It ain't right."

I heard the wheels screech, as Pap steered us back onto the freeway. And he near on crashed into a semi-truck that blared his horn at us.

"Here's a gov'ment that calls itself a gov'ment and lets on to be a gov'ment, and thinks it is a gov'ment, but it can't even be bothered to keep the people out ain't got no right to be here."

I squeezed the pillow tight on my head and started humming too just so's I could make his voice go away.

Me and Pap Get Sight of Los Angeles

"WAKE up. C'mon, wake up! There's somethin' I want you to see."

I heard him before I seen him. My eyes was closed on account I was sleeping. I warn't none too keen to open them up seeing as how he warn't in a very good humor the last time I heard from him. But I didn't have too much of a choice without I would pretend I was dead. So I opened up my eyes and there was Pap, staring in at me from a gap in the curtain. And his face was most normal, not like before. And I knowed right away that the good Pap was back, or at least as good as he could manage. He warn't above acting like a proper father from time to time, but it warn't very regular, and a body couldn't count on it.

"C'mon, son. I'm tellin' you it's a sight to see."

Well I clumb down from my bed and followed him outside around back to the ladder on the rear end of the camper. He told me to go first, and I clumb up that ladder and onto the roof of the camper, where I warn't normally allowed to go so only went there when Pap warn't around.

Now I must have slept most the entire day away, because the sun was a-setting and oh was it a pretty sight. We was out on top of a big hill, looking down on a whole bunch of twinkly lights.

"What'd I tell you. Los Angeles. Just like Alfonse said."

There was some mountains way out yonder, and the sun was just about set to disappear beneath 'em. And down below was a city that ran most as far as my eyes could see. It warn't a proper city like they learn you about in books, with skyscratchers all crammed right next to each other. It was more flat like, with long roads and highways with all sorts of cars and trucks and even motorcycles. You could see 'em all in a line with their headlights zipping along like shooting stars but on the ground. In Missouri they used to say there was full on twenty or thirty thousand people in Los Angeles, but I never believed it till I seen that wonderful spread of lights that still night when we first 'rrived.

Something about it got Pap to sentimentering. He reached out and put his hand on my shoulder. I tried not to flinch too much but I warn't accustomated to him touching me without which he was giving me a whupping.

"This is a new place. The bad times are all in the mirror now. We finally gonna get what's rightfully ours."

I looked up at him. Now, you prob'ly think I was a fool, and I prob'ly was. But he was my blood, and I didn't have noplace or nobody else to go to. So I guess I had a part inside me that was still a-hoping that maybe it was true this time.

"I'm a-gonna give up the bottle for good, Huck. I promise you. Just as soon as we get settled. Once I do this little job for Alfonse, we're a-gonna have more money than you ever dreamed of."

Well money don't mean much to me. From what I seen so far, folks with money got just as much worries as the rest of us, sometime even more. And I also knowed that money was like to make a body less inclined for 'venture. It was hard for me to see how a big pot of money would fix all of Pap's troubles. But maybe there was a chance. It sure did look sparkly from up atop that hill.

We camped by the side of the road. And I slept good, even though I'd slept most the whole day away. But it was the better kind of sleep. Instead of snakes and ghosts and all kinds of things like that, I dreamed about palm trees and the ocean and diamonds hanging from the sky.

In the morning, Pap used up the last of his cash to get some food, and he cooked up a nice and proper breakfast. There was bacon and eggs and toast and all such stuff as you would want on your first morning in Los Angeles.

Pap set acrossed from me and he was mighty communicable prob'ly on account of us finally arriving at our destination. "You're a Finn, boy, just like me." I knowed he was trying to say something nice, but I warn't sure how I felt about the comparable. "You take your whuppins like a man. I admire that."

I took another bite of bacon.

"We Finns we got pride. We don't need no one else. You see, everybody's out for themself. And there ain't no God who's gonna come in and make everything alright for us. If he exists—and that's a big if I say—he done forgot about us Finns way back yonder."

I knowed where he was going with this.

"Mama used to pray," I says. I didn't say it but I knowed that she even prayed for Pap. He didn't hear her do it but once, and she got a beating for it.

"Prayin's for the weakly," he says. "We ain't gonna sit around and feel sorry for ourselves. We gonna take what we need to get by in this world. We got each other, son. That's all we need."

I considered what he was saying. I was relucterant to throw my lot in with a person that had been so lowdown and mean. But, on the other hand, praying didn't get my mama anywhere 'cept dead and buried.

"You with me?"

Well I warn't ready to cut loose from him yet and I reckoned that it warn't no harm to give him another chance for a little while. So I says, "I'm with you." And I tried to make a smile when I said it. He was happy then, most like we was on the same team.

After we got done with our breakfast, Pap had some business to take care of, so he found an old phone booth out near a gas station. He was a-talking on the phone for quite a while, so I got to exploring and found a mound of dirt with a little hole at the top and there was big black ants a-coming in and out of the hole, so I knowed right away that it was an ant hill. I stuck my blade down in the hole and come up with about six or seven ants on it and I held 'em up real close to my eye so I could get a good look. And they was all confused like, running up and down a-wondering how they'd ended up a-dangling in the air when just a minute ago they was all cozy down in their ant home. Well one of 'em he run down my blade all the way onto my finger and I started to feel right sorry for him, 'cause I'd disturbed his peace and quiet. So I blowed him off nice and gentle, and he landed pretty near the door to his ant home, and he ran around and around a bit before he got orientated and ran back down the hole. Well that made me feel nice and warm inside, like I'd done a good turn.

"C'mon Huck. We're almost there."

Well Pap snuck up on me on account I'd been distractified by the ant hill. He was standing right over me, the top of his boots just about even with my head. And I got real lucky he didn't see my blade because I had it down near my shoes and I was able to push it under my leg before he seen it. As I said before, he warn't none too keen on anything that was my mama's, and I reckoned he'd take it away from me if he knowed I still kept holt of it.

As a way of celebrating, we pulled into a car wash, not the automatic kind where you drive through a tunnel of mops and brushes and soap gets sprayed all over your car and you'd better have your windows up without which you want to get wet and soapy. No, this was the kind where you pull in and they got a hose that only puts out water if you feed it some coins into its tiny little mouth. Pap had to hunt around but he found a couple of old quarters on the floor of the camper, and it was good enough to get us going. We sprayed all the dust and sand off the camper and she ended up looking shiny and new, and you'd most forget that she was old and beat-up and had come all the way from Missouri. And I could tell Pap was in a good mood, 'cause he used up the last few seconds to chase me 'round and 'round the camper a-spraying water and trying to get me wet. And he even let me splash him and was a-laughing and a-smiling instead of a-cursing. California was having a beneficent impact on his psychometry.

Well the sun was going down by now but Pap decided that we'd drive through the night so as to meet his business associate the next morning. And I fell asleep in the back.

CHAPTER 5

I Get Free from Pap
and Make a Friend

PAP'S good humor didn't last. I waked up the next morning to a kermotion that woulda brung Lazarus a-running and a-screaming from that cave of his. Pap was on a tear. I heard a bottle smash and break against the wall, and some of the pieces rained down on me. When I opened up my eyes, Pap was standing over me with a breaked bottle held high in his hand, like he had a notion to kill me dead.

"This was hers, wasn't it?"

Well now I seen what had happened. With his other hand he was holding my blade and—just as I suspected—it had set him off about my mama and had remembered him of some of the bad stuff that had happened atwixt them. I suppose that I had got a little loose with my ways and didn't hide it good before I went to sleep like I knowed I should. That always happens when there's good times. You loosen up a bit and it leaves a little gap where the bad times can creep back in again.

Well he jumped me good and got right up on top of me. He let go of the bottle—that was one good thing—but he used his free hand to clamp around my neck, which warn't such a good thing. I didn't answer his question on account I couldn't get any air out so I just tried to think about how I might get out of this if he really made an effort to kill me for real this time. He hadn't never quite got there before, but this Pap was awful mean and ornery and it warn't something I could rule out entirely.

"You have no right! She warn't no good, son. She warn't no good for us!"

He had the blade right up against my face, and I started wondering if he made to choke me to death or stab me to death.

"I told you I don't want none of her stuff around here no more. Nuthin. It ain't good for the neither of us. I oughta...." He paused for a minute, like he was trying to figger out what he oughta do. Well after a second he smacked me pretty good and it stung my cheek. But I was pretty relieved not to be stabbed or choked. I reckoned that Pap didn't really want to kill me because then he'd be all alone and wouldn't have nobody to yell at no more. Pap warn't his same self when he didn't have no one to yell at.

Well he clumb up off of me but I could see that he warn't done raging yet.

"If you ever cross me again, I swear I'll teach you who is who."

He made to break my blade and he slammed it down hard on the counter, but it was good and solid—like I said before—so it didn't break and just slid off the slick counter-top and Pap's hand got the worst of it. He yelled out and held up his hand and it was all bloody.

Well he was distractified now, and I seen that my blade had gotten away from Pap and was on the floor. I didn't think too much before I did it but I reached out to try and grab it and hide it before Pap noticed. But his foot come in and stepped on it before I could pick it up. I told you he was smart, and quick too.

"Nice try, boy," he says. And then he got all business-like. He picked up the blade and stuffed it in the trash bag. I warn't none too keen to see what he was gonna do next, 'cause that blade come from my mama and was one of the only things left in the world that had ever touched her hand. But I warn't in a good position to do anything about it right now.

Pap started gathering stuff up. First he went under the sink and reached way in the back and pulled out a little black satchel that I ain't never seen before. I'd explored most every little nook and crater of the camper but never once looked under there. And even in that moment I thunk to myself that I'd have to go in there and see what other truck he might be hiding. I seen that Pap held the bag like it was something important, like it was something that he'd never wanted me to see.

"I'm going out. Got some business to take care of. Don't you be sneakin' off again." By the way he looked at me, I could tell he was thinking that I warn't none too likely to follow directions. After a second, he says, "In fact, I'm gonna make sure you don't go nowhere."

So now I follow him—with my eyes—over to the driv-er's seat. He got down on his knees and pulled out a whole tangle of bun-gee cords. And I had an inkling of what he was a-gonna do. He slammed the door behind him as he left. Through the window, I could see him a-fixing those bun-gee cords to the camper in such a way as to keep the door real tight and closed, so I couldn't get out. And then I seen him do the same thing to the driver's door and t'one on the other side. I got a close-up look at his face, and he was smiling all satisfied, like he had pulled one over on me and was smarter than me. I seen him walk away, then, with the black satchel in his hands, but he shoved the bag of trash in one of those trash cans that you see on the sidewalk some time. I knowed then that, if I wanted my blade back, I'd have to get outta there somehow and get in that trash can.

After I couldn't see him no more, I got to working on the problem. First I went to the main door and tried to push against it real hard, hoping that maybe one of those bun-gees would come loose. But Pap had done a powerful good job of it. I did the same thing up at the front with the driver's door. But it warn't no use. They'd give a little, the doors, but the bun-gees was pulled tight and I knowed that I had to come up with a different type of solution to my predictament.

Well I walked up and down the camper from the front to the back and then back again because that was inclined to get me thinking good. Now I disremember how it come to me exactly but after a bit I found myself standing in the bathroom a-looking up at the ceiling. There was a fan up there, and I knowed that it was meant to blow air out. I clumb up from the toilet to the sink so's I could reach it and before you knowed it I had the fan off. Now it was just a hole right out to the sky, and I could see the clouds floating by. I thought, in just a minute or two I'm gonna be as free as those clouds. The hole warn't big enough for a grown man to go through but I can make myself pretty small and slithery when I want to, so I pulled myself right

up and through the hole. And—before you even knowed it—I was on the roof of the camper and then coming down that ladder on the back. My first priority was my blade. I went to the trash bin and I reached down in there and pulled it out. And boy was I happy. I was most ready to cry I was so happy, and well satisified with myself too for being smarter than Pap or at least as smart as him.

Now my satisfaction was disterrupted by the screech of some tires and a monstrous long car come tearing around a corner and near ran me over but then pulled in right next to the camper. The car warn't a new car, more like one of them policecop cars from a TV show that come on real late at night, 'cept it was plain brown and didn't have the markings of a policecop car. And the doors opened up and a whole bunch of men got out and they was loud and big and had drawings all over their arms, real bully drawings like snakes and dragons and skulls. Some kind of music was playing, only it warn't like proper music but had a funny rhythm to it and the guy warn't really singing but sort of half singing and half talking.

The men theyselves was black folk but also illegal Mexigrants, and they was wearing flashy sneakers with all sorts of colors, most like high-class women might wear when they get all dressed up like a peacock to go to a cockatiel party. One or two of 'em had basketballs, and they all went straight onto the court and started shooting and somebody set up a big radio where they could play the same kind of music as was coming out their car just a minute ago. Now I watched 'em for a time—through the fence—and they was an awful sight to watch, being able to jump so high and bounce the ball so quick like. It went pretty good until one guy pushed another guy, and then the guy who got pushed threw a punch and then the game had to stop until they could pull those guys away from one t'other.

I decided that this must be Los Angeles proper because it had the feel of a city with people and cars everywhere. But I didn't see no sign of the palm trees or the ocean, so I reckoned I should look around and find out where they might be. I went a-wandering to explore. But exploring in Los Angeles was a bit different than the woods back home. I tried to make to cross the street, but it seemed to stretch on forever and the cars was driving quick and some of the drivers was looking down and not looking up, so they wouldn't pay me no tension at all. So I had to go up to the interstection where there was a light, even though I warn't in the habit of waiting for a green light.

Well I noticed that there warn't nobody who looked normal regular like me, but there was lots of the Mexigrants and some black folk sprinkled in too. But it was contrary to the way that Pap told me, 'cause they all seemed to get along just fine and didn't pay no tension to each other, without which you count the two guys who was fighting on the basketball court. I did see one sight that was dreadful and strange. It was a couch laying out near the street, but it was in bad shape, and there was a man on it. He was most dead asleep and didn't notice me much. He looked like he was sick maybe, and there was scratches on his arm. I didn't know why but right aways I felt sorry for him, even though I hadn't never met him before and didn't really know anything 'bout his circumstantials. I even tried to wake him up so as to help him get to a better place, but he was relucterant, and so I gave up after a time.

I crossed the street and went over to a smaller street, just walking and looking. There was rows and rows of tiny little houses that was packed close to each other. I seen one or two palm trees, but they was sorry palm trees and not as tall as a mountain as Pap said. The houses had grass out front, but it was most dead and brown, 'cept one house where there was a Mexigrant standing out front with a water hose a-watering his grass and it looked green like proper grass.

He nodded at me and he says, *"Hola, buenos dias. ¿Cómo*

45

está usted?" He was talking like a proper Mexigrant and not like the man who gave me the tacos in the desert. I says hullo back to him and smiled, but he prob'ly didn't understand what I was driving at.

I come to another corner and now my nose started taking the lead and drawing me to the left. Up ahead I seen a crowd of people gathered 'round a big barrel with smoke coming out and I reckoned that I had come up on a barbecue of some sort. I made myself slithery again and wiggled my way through all them bodies that was waiting for food and I got up real close where I could see all that meat a-sizzling on the grill and my stomach near jumped out my mouth. And there was saliver gathering in my mouth most like I was one of them dogs that Pavlov kept starving in their cages till they couldn't hardly stand it no more.

I stuffed my hands in my pockets and realized that I was running short of assets that I could easily liquefy. So I did what any reasonable person should do in a situation like that and I waited until the man turned his back to get more meat and then I borrowed a rack of ribs. Pap always said it warn't no harm to borrow things if you was meaning to pay them back some time. I reckoned it warn't nuthin but a soft name for stealing, but there's times a body's just got to eat.

I got outta there pretty quick and went on with my exploring. Pretty soon I come up on another long fence and on the other side was all sorts of kids a-yelling and a-playing and raising hell. Well I knowed right away that this was recess time and these California kids was in school. I didn't care too much for school, but the recess was one part that I could see some profit in. These particular kids seemed most like kids back home. There was some girls all standing alone and trading in some sort of trinkets. And there was a whole bunch of 'em playing kickball, which is kinda like baseball 'cept there's a big red rubber ball that you kick instead of hit with a bat.

I watched for a time and right away here come a ball into the corner a-right where I was standing, and the fielder—a real skinny-looking black kid—come a-bounding over to scoop it up. He hurled it back in and I noticed right away that he had a good way with the ball.

"Nice throw," I says.

"Thanks," he says. He stopped and payed me some tension now. It seemed he might have been puzzling about why I was on t'other side of the fence.

"Hey you got ribs?"

"I reckon yes."

"From the place down the corner?"

"Yep."

"Oh man I love those things."

Well I warn't inclined to part with any of 'em, but sometime you got to give something up in order that you might make a friend, which is worth it even though it don't sound like it.

"You want some?" I says, and I offered him one through the fence, and he went right in on it.

"I'm Tom," he says with his mouth full and his face all red with sauce. "Tom Sawyer." I supposed that I prob'ly looked a similar mess.

"I'm Huckleberry."

"Never heard of a name like that before."

"Mos' folks jus' call me Huck." Well just then a bell rung out loud and shrill acrossed the yard, and all them kids start running back into the school. Tom Sawyer he looked back over his shoulder for a second, but then he turned back to me.

"You coming to school, Huck?"

"I ain't got much inclination for book-learning." And it was true.

"What you got an inclination for?"

"Bank robbing. Piracy. 'Venture." I was stretching a bit there, but I could tell that he was the kind that would appreciate such things as those.

Tom Sawyer he looked back again. There was a lady at the door a kind of ushering the kids back into the school and she seen him from way far off.

"Mr. Sawyer!" she yells. "You heard that bell! Get back in here, son!" And then she turned to try and break up two boys who had started shoving each other in the line. Well Tom Sawyer he seen that she was distractified and he ran to a spot nearby, where the fence was pulled up a little bit.

"You gonna help me?"

Having recently achieved my freedom from my Pap, I was mighty pleased to be able to help another boy achieve freedom for his own self. So I got down on my knees and I helped pry him out through that gap in the fence. By the time the teacher lady looked up for Tom Sawyer again, we was long gone. I'll bet she was mighty confuzzled about where he went off to.

CHAPTER 6

Me and Tom Sawyer Most Get Killed by a Gangster

TOM Sawyer said that we was in a place called Compton, which warn't a proper part of Los Angeles but an even better part if you was looking for 'venture. I told him that the best place for 'venturing back home was down by the river. So he takes me up on a bridge and says he'll show me the river they got. Well it warn't like no river that I'd ever seen before. There warn't no trees or mud but just gray concrete in kinda like a V shape. And there was just a bit of water, like you might find in a creek, not like a proper river. But there was something beautiful and nice about it anyway. It ran right under the road, and it most seemed like nobody even noticed it, even though it was right out in the open. It seemed like a place where a body could go if they didn't want no one to bother with 'em.

"My Aunt Polly," Tom says, "she says that this water starts up in the mountains—" he pointed off up north where there was some mountains a way far off "—and dripped and dribbled all the way down here on the way to the Pacific Ocean."

"She's a scientist, your aunt?"

"A lawyer. But that don't mean that she don't know about rivers and stuff like that. She's just about the smartest person I ever met. She sure is. You know what's out there in the ocean, right?"

I didn't know.

"Pirates." Well I shoulda thought of that.

My eyes followed the river down until it disappeared way down below us. I reckoned that the ocean was out that way and I hoped I'd get to see it one day and maybe meet some real live pirates. And then I struck another idea, so I says to Tom, "The river we got back home has got critters and stuff. Birds and muskrats and coons."

"Follow me," he says. And I did. We went down under the bridge and cut through another fence and then we was a-scampering down the concrete walls of the river—they was kinda slanted like—and we went down until we was in the water up to our knees.

"Look close," Tom says. "There's some critters down here."

Well I took my blade out and I started lifting up rocks and other stuff as I found in the river. Tom Sawyer was hunting too and pretty soon he pulled up an old rusted license plate that was from Utah and I told Tom that it was a bully find and just as good as anything that me and Ben Rogers ever found in old Mrs. Loftus's witch bin. Tom Sawyer was the kind of fellow that old Ben woulda liked if he hadn't been so far away back home.

It warn't long before I seen what Tom was talking about. There was crawfish in the river, and I stabbed one good with my blade and held it up for Tom to see. He was a-wiggling and trying to get me with his claws, and I couldn't hardly blame him. But it warn't long before he started slowing down on account he was dying. Tom was keen on my blade and said it was real dope, which was his way of saying that it was bully. I know it's powerful strange, but that's how boys talk in Los Angeles.

"You ever been to a crawfish boil?" I asked Tom. But he didn't know what I was a-driving at. "That's where you stick a bunch of these crawfish in a pot and boil 'em up until they die. And then you open 'em up and eat their guts with all sorts of spices and mop up the juice with bread."

"You eat those things?"

He couldn't hardly believe it when I told him that I ate fourteen—that's two more than a full dozen—last Fourth of July. He said it was disgustable and not right, but I knowed that he'd eat just as many, prob'ly more, if they was prepared right and set down in front of him.

Well after that we had a smoke down under one of them bridges over the river, and it was awful pleasurable to discover that a boy here in California might enjoy the same kind of activity as we did back home in St. Petersburg. Smokin's a monstrous good way to make a new friend or to come closer with a friend you already got. If you haven't tried it yet, you'll see when you do. You don't even neither have to say nuthin to each other, and Tom Sawyer and me was mostly quiet while we was smoking.

After a time we started in to exploring again. We clumb up a fence to get on t'other side where there was a building most dead and abandoned. Tom Sawyer said that he had been avoiding it on account there was rumors that the building was a-haunted but that he reckoned atwixt the two of us we could fight off any ghosts or ghouls that might make an appearance.

Tom breaked a window on the first floor, and we clumb up through the hole, being careful not to scrap ourselves up on the glass. I followed Tom Sawyer up to the second floor. It was dark inside 'cept for little splinters of light that come in through cracks in the walls. And it smelled something like the cave back home but different too, like there was things growing on the walls. It was so strange and quiet I got a real case of the fantods.

But Tom Sawyer warn't afeard at all no more. He come a-screaming out from the shadows.

"Surrender now and I won't make you walk the plank!"

I seen now that he had a big piece a wood in his hands a-waving it like a saber, so I grabbed one too and we got to fighting real good with our sabers. Clack, clack! He parried me good, but I made to block him even better.

"You'll get three years in the brig!" Tom says. "You'll be eating scraps from the galley and carving your story into the wall with a butter knife."

He was a-coming at me pretty good and I was backing up, trying to fend him off. And I suppose I got distractified by the story he was telling too. So pretty soon I tripped over something on the floor. Tom Sawyer he quit talking real abrupt.

"Well don't stop now," I says. "It's a bully speech and you was just getting going."

But Tom didn't say nuthin. He was looking at something behind me. I turned and most fainted. There was a shriveled-up hand right up close to my face. It was sticking out from under a blanket or some such and me and Tom knowed right away that we was dealing with a dead body. I had fallen right atop of him during our saber fight. Well it didn't take me but half a second to get up off of him. Tom Sawyer and me was mighty quiet for a time out of respect for the dead of course. All we could see was the hand on account of he was covered by the blanket and his clothes. His hand didn't look human no more but more like a witch's hand, and we couldn't neither tell if it was a regular man or a black man or a Mexigrant.

Finally Tom says, "How long you think he's been here?"

"Dunno," I says. Finally I got overcome with curiopathy so I got down close to him again and used my blade to pull back a part of the blanket. Well I ain't even gonna try to explain what we saw where his face used to be. It warn't something that a body can't never forget. Tom Sawyer ain't one to look away from anything but I seen him look away too.

We might a been a-frozen there forever but we was awoken up by a noise. There was a clatter somewheres and there was echoes. Then voices. Not the kind where you can understand what they're saying but the kind where you knows that you're not alone no more. The voices was low and short, more like a man than a woman, and angry too, not friendly like.

Tom and me we left the dead body to hisself and went creeping to the stairs, and we could tell that the voices was coming from one floor down. We slinked down the stairs real quiet-like and pretty soon the voices become more clear.

The first one I heard says, "I didn't mean nuthin by it!"

And my ears most jumped offa my head. It was Pap's voice, I was sure. I didn't say nuthin to Tom right then but kept it to myself. But Tom he must've seen that something was a-bothering me, 'cause he says to me. "What is it? What's wrong?" But he said it like a whisper.

Like I says, I didn't answer him right off but kept coming down the stairs until I kind of hid myself behind a wall, but I peeked around to see what I could see. Tom Sawyer was behind me a bit, waiting for a signal.

Right away I seen that I heard it correct. It was Pap alright, and he was in a dire predictament. There was two men—Mexigrants—holding guns that was pointed straight at him. Pap he was pollergizing with all the might he could muster.

"I got nuthin against you people."

"I should think not," says one of the Mexigrants. He was dressed up all nice like he was a senator or a funeral director, and I reckoned he was one of the new boss Mexigrants that Pap was always talking about. "I should think not. Seeing as how you've entered into a contract of sorts. And seeing how my family's been in this country for 150 years. Here in California we don't typically start our business transactions with ethnic slurs. It's considered uncouth."

Well he talked real smooth like that with big words, and I reckoned that he was upset about something that Pap had said to him. Pap had a way of getting up under your skin with his way of talking, especially for people that hadn't gotten used to his ways yet. But this Mexigrant was playing it nice and easy.

"Should I put a cap in him, Jefe?" That was the other Mexigrant. This one looked different. He had drawings all 'round his neck and face and big round things in his ears. And he wore sunglasses even though it was dark enough to be night in there. And just a T-shirt, not a fancy get-up with a jacket.

"Not so fast, Ivan," says Jefe. "I am still quite interested to sample the backwoods victuals."

He looks at Pap. But Pap don't understand.

"The drugs, Mr. Finn. Please give the drugs to

my associate."

Pap he stiffened up then. "What about the money?"

"Yes, the money. Ivan's got it right here." I seen that Ivan was carrying a briefcase. "But, you see," says Jefe, "you're really not in much of a position to demand anything right now."

Ivan went up to Pap and grabbed the satchel out of his hands, pretty rough-like, so Pap didn't have no choice but to let go.

"But that's the deal. Alfonse said...."

Pap didn't even bother a-finishing his sentence. Jefe ignored him and opened up the satchel. He stuck his finger in and then tasted a little bit of the stuff that was in there. He got real pleasant and relaxified then.

"Mmmm... Mr. Finn, I'm happy to report that your manners belie the quality of your product."

"So you'll give me the money?"

I seen clear that Pap didn't fully understand the particularities of his situation.

"I think we're ready to complete this transaction."

Jefe raised his gun and pointed it straight at Pap. And Ivan did just the same, like he was copying Jefe.

"No, no," says Pap and it was near on the first time I seen him scared for real. "We had a deal."

"Pap," I says but I only whispered. Tom Sawyer had crept up beside me and he heard me say it. From his eyes I could tell that he understood the seriosity.

"Now, Jefe?"

"Yes, now." We watched Jefe turn and fire. BANG! But it warn't Pap who fell. It was Ivan. He dropped to the floor and dropped his gun too. Pap looked like he had wet hisself or worse.

"I'm really sorry that you had to get embroiled in all of this, Mr. Finn." Jefe walked over and looked down at Ivan who he'd just shot. There was blood coming out of him and making a big pool, but he warn't dead yet. "I've recently learned that Ivan is quite the up-and-comer at the LAPD."

He kicked the gun on the floor and it went spinning off. I suppose he wanted to get rid of it, but it come spinning out of the darkness right toward me and Tom. I most jumped to see a gun that close.

"Don't worry, Mr. Finn. Despite your lack of multicultural awareness…" Jefe got down on top of Ivan, "…I have every intention of giving you your money. Just tell Alfonse that I'll be expecting another shipment next month."

Now Tom Sawyer whispers to me, "That's your dad? He's a gangster?" Not knowing Pap, Tom had formed a high 'pinion of him already. That's how it is sometime when you're jus' getting familiar with a thing, you get to forming a feeling that might not match up with how things really are. I done it many time myself.

Now Jefe was making to kill Ivan dead. He ripped open his shirt and inside—all taped up to his stomach— was a machine that was recording all the talk. Jefe ripped it off, and Ivan yelped a little bit.

"They'll be here in five minutes," says Ivan, breathing hard and heavy. "You're going to rot in jail. *Jefe.*" He said that last word in a different way than he'd said it before and it made everyone know that he didn't like that word.

"You hear that, Mr. Finn? The authorities are on their way. We'd best be going. Ivan says we've got five minutes, but I'm guessing it's ten at least." Jefe smiled most like he was handing a bowkay of flowers to a pretty girl. "Plenty of time for me to show him my appreciation for his loyalty."

Jefe put his gun down and bent over and clamped his hands right around Ivan's neck. And I finally decided that now was the time to make my presence appreciated.

"Hey get offa him," I says.

Boy did they jump! I come up so quiet that I was most right on top of them before they even noticed. Of course I'd picked up Ivan's gun too on account I didn't trust neither one of 'em. Pap couldn't help hisself and he says "Huck?" out of how surprised he was. But that warn't none too smart, 'cause then Jefe got an idea of what was going on.

"You know this kid?" he asks Pap.

But I don't let Pap answer and I jus' repeat myself. "Get up offa him." I reckoned that if there was one good guy in the bunch—and I warn't sure of that neither—it was Ivan. I grabbed Jefe's gun and handed it back to Tom Sawyer who was right behind me.

Well Jefe got up alright and he come right at me, smiling.

"Give me the gun, kid. You're not going to shoot me."

"How'd you get in here, son?" Pap continued to misunderestimate his situation. "You got good timing."

"This is your son?" Jefe says. "I'll be damned. Bringing a child to a drug deal. This is what I get for doing business with bumpkins."

Now Jefe gets all serious with Pap. "Tell your son to put the gun down, Mr. Finn."

"Shut up with your Mr. Finn business. Tables are turned now. I don't got to put up with this uppity talk from a Mexigrant."

Jefe's face went all dark now, like he was real angry. "You're going to regret this, Mr. Finn. I've shown a good deal of patience with—." But he was disterrupted by a siren somewheres out in the streets. From the sound of it, it was still a ways off, but I wouldn't a minded if they'd been there ten minutes ago.

Now it was Pap's turn to make a play. "C'mon, son. Let's get out here. We're rich now." But I swung the gun 'round and pointed it right at him. I dunno why I done it. He was my Pap, you're right, but I wanted to be free of him, I guess, and I was beginning to see how I might be able to fernagle it.

"Son, give me the gun." He said it like to scare me with thoughts of another whupping. But it didn't work 'cause I had a gun.

"No," I says. "Don't move."

"You slimy little toad. I'm gonna—" He was jus' about ready to kill me dead, if the situation warn't so turned around on him. And then he looked at Ivan's briefcase. "I'm a-takin' the money."

"I said don't move." And I said it strong, so as he would know that I warn't playing. And all of us we could hear the sirens getting louder. Well Pap he up and ran without the money. Afore we knowed it, he was outta sight and all we could hear was the echo of his footprints. And I suppose you're right, I coulda shot him in the back instead of letting him get away, but he was still my Pap and I warn't inclined to do it. I guess I payed a big price down the line for that little bit of sentimentering.

Jefe was still being covered by Tom Sawyer, but I turned back to give him another gun to look at. He recovered real nice, and he smiled at us, all dignified like. "Now this is a fine predicament, boys." He said it nice, like we was his friends, but that was just for show.

"This is so dope!" says Tom Sawyer. "I never caught a gangster before!"

And then the policecops come.

CHAPTER 7

I Get Adoptered Out to Some Thespians

WHEN the day come, the lawyers got me all dressed up so as to make the jury think that I was a good boy, all dismal regular and decent. I was mighty uncomfortable, and my shoes they made a clomping sound that woulda

scared off a bear. They called my name and I had to walk into a little wooden box and swear on the Bible that I warn't gonna lie. Then they told me to point to the man who shot and killed Ivan. They called Ivan "Lieutentant Rodriguez" 'cause that was his real name and not the fake one that he used to hocus Jefe. He ended up dying 'ventually so the trial was all about the murder. I did it just like they wanted me to and didn't have to lie 'cause it really was Jefe who done it. Jefe most looked like he was bored the whole time and didn't even say hullo to me. Tom Sawyer was there, and his Aunt Polly too. And right away I seen that he was right about her. She was beautiful and intelligenic and Tom was awful lucky to have an aunt like that.

Now after I was done they put me in the back of a big long limousine like I was a movie star or such like. The seats was all shiny leather and there was gadgets and gizmos all over, most like a spaceship. I pressed one button and a drawer opened up with snacks and drinks and such truck as I woulda paid a million dollars for when I lived out in the lean-to. I tried another little lever and all of a sudden a window opened up, but this window warn't on the side but on the ceiling. I clumb up on the seat and stuck my head out. Tom Sawyer and his Aunt Polly was on the sidewalk and I waved to him, but his Aunt Polly pulled him away. Everyone had formed the general 'pinion that there warn't no good that could come about from me and Tom Sawyer staying friends, seeing how we'd gotten our-selves all tangled up in a murder on the first day we met. Me and Tom thought it had all worked out pretty good—for everybody 'cept Ivan. But Aunt Polly was in the other camp, and I can't hardly blame her. That's how it is when you get older. No matter how intelligenic you are, there's just no talking sense into you on certain subjects.

And then I seen the Judge coming toward the limo.

The judge in the case was a Judge Thatcher, who was

maybe the tallest man you'd ever seen. He was a black man and he had a white beard that made him look kind and wise, most like God in one of them old drawings. And Judge Thatcher he took an interest in me, most grandfather-like. When he got in the car, he told me to close the skylamp—that was the proper name for the window on the ceiling—and that he wanted to talk to me a bit. He told the driver to go ahead and we started driving, but I didn't know where yet until the Judge got done telling me his plan.

He 'splained that Jefe was judged guilty and would be in jail for a long time and maybe even never get out, so he warn't gonna come after me. Then he said that Jefe had hurt a lot of people and that the gov'ment was mighty keen to get him and had put up a reward for putting him in jail. And he said that what Tom Sawyer and I had done was real brave and that we rightly deserved that reward which was two hundert thousand dollar. I reckoned that was an awful sight of money, and Judge Thatcher said that me and Tom we'd split it and that he'd hold onto it for me until I was ready to go to college and get a proper education. Now I didn't say nuthin to the Judge, on account he was trying to be so nice and kind, but I warn't too keen on spending them spoils on an education. It seemed to me that the whole point of captivating a bad guy and collecting a bunch of reward money was so that you wouldn't *have* to be cooped up all day a-listening to other folks talk and instead could go have 'ventures and explore and not worry too much about book-learning. But the Judge had a different angle on it, I guess. He kept talking and told me an idea he had for where I would go next.

"Now normally, in a situation like this, when a young man's parents are nowhere to be found, he might be placed in a foster home somewhere in the city. But I've got an idea that you might like it a bit more where there's some room to roam, where there's trees and rocks to climb, and horses too."

You see, the 'thorities had still been looking for Pap but he'd made hisself scarce if he was still in Los Angeles, and they warn't inclined to let me run off to the woods on my own, though that woulda been just fine by me. The Judge tells me that he knows a couple of nice ladies who don't have no kids of their own and they live out in the country where I'd maybe be more comfortable. Well, it's hard to have a firm 'pinion on something that you don't know nuthin about, but the Judge made it sound awful bully and I reckoned that I could get free if I wanted to, so there warn't no harm in a-trying it out.

For a time, me and the Judge was quiet. That's how it is with people you like, you don't have to be talking all the time and can just let the time pass like you was alone out under the stars. I stared out the window and watched all the cars go by. I couldn't 'magine where they'd all be going. One time I seen a camper most like Pap's, and my 'magination got going and I started thinking that he was a-following us just to come get me back. But then I seen another camper and another one too, and I reckoned that it warn't true and that I was near on permanent safe with the Judge. You see, I'd been with Pap so long that it warn't so easy to let go of the thought of him.

That's what I told myself in my brain. Now after I tell you the whole story, you may think that I shoulda been a little bit more worried, and not so easy to think that I was free of Pap for good. But I can't hardly blame myself, 'cause the future always looks different after it becomes the past.

It seemed like we most drove forever. The sun went down and hid itself behind the mountains and the cars got fewer and fewer the longer we went. Pretty soon we was off the highway and just on streets going up and up and up toward the mountains. And then it come full dark and you couldn't neither see the mountains no more even though they was still there. The Judge said it was a special place and named it Bell Canyon. That's how it is in Los Angeles, they got all sorts of names for the different parts, even though it's all one place.

The limousine turned up a long driveway and we turned one way and then t'other before we got to the house. And oh what a house. It most looked like a palace where a king would live or maybe a duke if he was one of the top dukes. There was a monstrous tall fountain out front that pushed the water up in the air and when it fell down it made a slapping sound. I jumped out of the car just about as soon as we stopped, leaving the Judge behind, and right away there was a lady. She was coming out of the house on account she was greeting us. Well right away she learned me her name was Ms. Douglas, and she was one of the ladies I was gonna live with. Her hair was mostly gray-like and she was awful old, prob'ly forty years or older if you asked me. But she wears her hair back in a donkeytail, just like a little girl. She had the nicest smile on when she said hullo to me, so I smiled nice and I says thank you even before she invited me inside.

I got to meet Miss Watson next. She was the second lady who lived there, and she was younger and come from Japan or there-a-parts. They had cooked up a special meal just for me and the Judge, and we all set down at the table like a proper family. The Judge he said a prayer and Miss Watson grabbed my hand so that everybody was a-holding hands while he prayed. Well I was mighty uncomfortable but it didn't do for me to make a fuss, so I just pulled my hand away when he was done. The food was spaghetti which is one of my top favorites, so I jumped in and didn't stop until my stomach was crammed full with spaghetti, which was after a long time. The ladies and the Judge, they ate slow-like on account they was done growing, and they talked about stuff that people in California talk about, like the rains a-coming and how many roads the Judge was gonna take to get back to his home, even though he warn't the one driving.

I got awful bored after a time so I asked if I could use the bathroom and Ms. Douglas pointed where to go. My main purpose in going was to explore a little bit and decide if this warn't the type of place where a body could live for a while. The first thing I seen, on the wall, was a whole bunch of photograms of Ms. Douglas and Miss Watson. They was wedding-type pictures, and the Judge was there, so right away I figgered out that those two ladies must be married to each other and the Judge done did it for 'em. It's strange, I know, but that's how it is in California.

I clumb up the stairs and found the bathroom but first I looked in one of the bedrooms and saw that the bed was near covered in so many pillows you coulda had a sleepover for all your friends and their friends too, and you'd still have pillows left to spare. In the bathroom, it smelled most like a parfumery, and there was pretty little soaps in the shapes of seashells. Well, you can see from what I'm describing that these two ladies was dismal regular and decent. It warn't to my personal style. Well on my way down the stairs I run straight into Ms. Douglas, and she said that she wanted to show me to my room. It turned out that bedroom with all those pillows was the same bedroom where they wanted me to stay.

After a time the Judge left and I got myself ready for sleep. Ms. Douglas helped me put all those pillows on the floor. At the end I was most buried 'neath a mound of blankets, and Ms. Douglas stood at the door, most like she was my mama or some such.

"Goodnight, Huckleberry."

"Goodnight, Ms. Douglas."

"Don't you worry, we'll turn this into a boy's room soon enough."

I told her I warn't worried about it, but I must admit I warn't right comfortable. She left me alone and I guess I tried to fall asleep but it was downright difficult in that bed that was so high and tall and that wanted to swallow me up it was so soft, even without the pillows. I warn't in the habit of sleeping like that. Well I laid there for as long as I could stand it but it warn't for me. I seen that the moon was shining in the window good and bright, so I got up to take a look and right away I noticed that there was a big old oak tree that was growing right up on the house. If the window was open, I reckoned that I could reach out and touch it.

I know you already guessed it, but I'm gonna tell it to you anyway. I went straight out that window and I got my hands on one of the branches of the oak tree. When I first opened the window, I says to myself that I'm only just exploring and that I'll climb back up the tree once I'm ready to sleep. But by the time I clumb down to the ground, I had made up my decision that I warn't gonna stay. Those ladies seemed nice enough, and it wouldn't do for a person like me to horn in on it. I reckoned that I was free of Pap now and that it wouldn't do to give up my freedom so quick and easy like.

Well, I seen that their house butted right up against the mountain, but it warn't a proper mountain and more like jus' a hill. If I got up over the hill, I could get a good start and get off into the woods or maybe even back to the proper part of the city. I seen a path leading up toward the mountain and I was just about there when I heard a sound. It was the sound a horse makes. I looked back and I seen another building behind the house, kind of set off a ways. There was no lights on in the house, but I seen a light down there by t'other building. And I got to remember that the Judge said there was horses out here, not like the city.

Okay, I says to myself, I'm a-gonna go take a look at these horses before I go up over this mountain. But I'm a-gonna do it quick, so as not to admit for a delay. When

I got close to the horse building, I made myself real quiet, and I could hear the sounds of a radio—it was a baseball game—and some horse noises too. I peeked around a corner to see what I was getting into, and I seen him there before he seen me. A Mexigrant. He was wearing a baseball hat like to keep the sun out of your eyes, only it was nighttime. He was a-sweeping and a-whistling too. But then he seen me.

"Hullo," I says.

"*Hola muchacho*," he says back. "Busting out already?"

I didn't really answer him.

"I don't blame you. It's a big world out there. Hate to be cooped up, like these horses here."

"You work for Ms. Douglas?"

He nodded. "I keep the stables clean, *muchacho*. Tend to the horses."

I looked over and saw the most beautiful horse I ever seen. She was watching us.

"Carolina," the Mexigrant says. "She would like a treat." He throws me an apple and I catched it good and solid. I held it out to her but she got nervous on account she didn't know that I was Huck. She jumped up a couple time and made a ruckus. So the Mexigrant talked to her in his own language.

"*Mansita, mansita, Carolina. No te alborotes. Esta bien. Tranquila, niña.*" Well she must have learned how to speak Mexigrant 'cause she went quiet awful quick. When I held out my hand, she snatched up the apple with her teeth, and she crunched it up all in one bite. I could even see her tongue. The Mexigrant told me that Carolina liked it when a body rubs her nose. So I tried that and she did like it.

"It's a shame you're leaving so soon. I could use some help." I knowed he was trying to put the hocus on me to make me stay, but I didn't mind.

"You live here?" I asked him. He took me 'round back of the horse building and showed me the little room where he slept.

"*Asi es, muchacho*. Until my family can be with me. Close enough to comfort the horses when they get spooked by a *coyote*." He said it all most regular, 'cept the last word that he said like a Mexigrant. We had coyotes back home and I started thinking how it might not be comfortable for me to run into a pack of them up on the mountain.

I pointed at a photogram on the wall. It was a Mexigrant woman and a little girl, a Mexigrant too.

"My daughter," he says. "A little bit younger than you now. They are in Arizona now. But they will come to be with me." He pulled the photogram down and looked at it close, most like they was right there in the room with us. "As soon as we have enough money." He put the picture back where it was.

"It is good to be close to the horses. Carolina—she is an early riser. *Una madrugadora*." He picked up his broom and started sweeping again. "Better hurry, *muchacho*. They're gonna set out after you when they find your bed is empty." He was hocusing me again.

"Or you could stick around for breakfast tomorrow. Miss Watson—her omelets are the best. *Muy ricos*."

I ain't one to philosopher-size but I took to turning the issue over and around in my brain. There warn't much use in thinking that I might live there with them ladies and become a family. It's rough living in a house with folks so dismal regular and decent. But then I reckoned that maybe there might be some value in delaying my departure and that I might could turn it to my 'vantage.

"I am Miguel," he says to me and we shook our hands together.

CHAPTER 8

Miguel Learns Me to Be a Charro

WELL the next day Ms. Douglas took me into town. She wanted to get me some proper clothes, even though I told her that I didn't want none. There was restaurants everywhere, most like four or five on every corner, and it seemed to me that California people must not know how to cook for theyselves. I asked Ms. Douglas about it and she said that it was on account of everybody being so busy all the time with work and school and such. Well it seemed to me that the California people had it all wrong if they was putting things like work and school before the important stuff like getting a good meal at home.

But she took me through the drive-by, and I ordered pizza and a hamburger and four tacos. It's right what people say about California—that there are so many people there you can eat just about anything from anywhere in the world, and sometimes you don't even have to get out of your car.

She took me to a shopping market that was so big it went on for miles and miles. Inside there was every kind of thing you could ever want plus a lot stuff that you'd never ever want. And there was tinkly music playing everywhere and everything was so clean and white it made you feel all sleepy and ready to buy stuff, if you had money in your pocket. I didn't have money but Ms. Douglas told me that she was gonna get me some stuff that a boy like me would like to have.

But I didn't see too much stuff to my liking. There was one store that had blue jeans that looked about right— they had holes in all the right places and you could tell they'd been left there by a boy who'd knowed how to have fun—but Ms. Douglas said they was near on a million bucks, and I thought well maybe I can get rich by selling my old dirty jeans. But then I remembered how all the holes had got there, and I got to sentimentering about my 'ventures with Ben Rogers along the big river, and I figgered that I'd keep my jeans and they could keep their million dollars, 'cause I was the only one who could best appreciate the holes that I'd made myself. And I felt bad for the boy who'd left his jeans in that store, even if somebody did give him a million dollars, because some other body was enjoying the holes that he hisself had made.

There was one store that had all kinds of gadgets and gizmos. Ms. Douglas let me stay there a long while, 'cause she had some female shopping to do. There was a monstrous wall of TVs there, some of 'em as big as a car, and you wouldn't believe how much different stuff was on the screen. There was policecops and robbers and a show about aeroplanes and people talking all the time about all such stuff as people care about, which is a lot.

There was a channel that called itself a sports channel and I got all excited to see what they'd have on there. But after a while it got tiresome, 'cause they didn't actually show any sports on there, but jus' people arguing and yelling about sports. Well my experience with Pap had given me a disinclination to hear people yell all the time, so I kept a-going. There was a music channel that didn't have no music, and there was a science channel that didn't have proper science but just explosives all the time. After a time I found a TV with the policecops and robbers on and watched that for a while. It was a bully good show, 'cause the good guys was real good and the bad guys was right bad. And the good guys had an attitude for science and had all sorts of gizmos they used to find the bad guys.

Then I got to watching this one other channel where there was two fellows talking on a stage. Well the one fellow he was talking about how the A-rabs was a-coming for all of us with bombs and guns and we'd better watch out. And the Mexigrants was gonna take all our jobs, just like Pap said. Also the homersexuals was bad too and they might take all our children and convert 'em to all sorts of bad stuff. Well it sounded pretty bad to me. But the next fellow said that the first fellow he had it all wrong and that instead there was gonna be floods and fires and tornadoes that was gonna kill us all dead. And, in the meanwhile, he said all the rich folks was all the time a-plotting and a-scheming how to take the money of the regular man and put him in the poorhouse. And that—if the rich folks didn't get it first—then it would be the Chinamen who would take all our money and all our land and take it back to China with 'em. Well that sounded pretty bad too, and I got to feeling down about the whole situation of the world. Why, a body could go about enjoying life and having certain 'ventures and he wouldn't have any idea that there was so much to be afeard of. So I kept watching and trying to keep track of all the things or people that might kill me dead or take all my stuff, but then after a while my 'pinion changed and I seen what they was really up to.

You see, these fellows was making out to disagree but they was really playing a game and they was on the same team in a way. They was making out that the world was gonna end, without which we put one of them in charge, and each one was hoping that maybe we'd pick him and not the other guy. So maybe there was some truth in what they was sayin' or maybe not, but you can never tell what the truth is exactly when someone is trying to hocus you. It's like that time that Ben Rogers told me there was a shark in the river so as I'd come running down fast, only when I got there it was just a dead mud turkle.

Ms. Douglas come back after a while, and it was good 'cause I'd had my fill of television for a while. She did buy me some clothes then. They warn't quite as stiff as the clothes they made me wear for the Judge but still a lot more stiff than I normally like. But I pretended to like 'em real good, seeing as how Ms. Douglas was so keen to do me a good turn.

When we got home, though, I went back to my old clothes that made me feel comfortable like. Miguel was out at the stables, and he acted like he was 'specting to see me. I guess Miss Watson had been out riding Carolina, and now she—Carolina, I mean, not Miss Watson—needed a proper bath. Miguel showed me how to take the burrs out of her tail and then he gave me a hose to use to wash her good. It was most like washing Pap's camper, 'cept that Carolina was a living critter and you could tell she liked being under the water. There was even a squeegee type thing that we used to get the water offa her but Miguel called it a sweat scraper. It gave me a powerful good feeling to make her clean, which was strange because I warn't too keen on being clean myself.

"You are a natural, *muchacho*," Miguel told me. "A real *charro*." That's how it was with Miguel. He could make a body feel good just by smiling and saying something in Mexigrant that you'd never understand in a million year. He told me that he was real busy taking care of all of the horses and that he wanted my help with taking care of Carolina in particularity. He said it would take some of my time but that it would help Ms. Douglas and Miss Watson and that it would make Carolina happy too. I told him that it was bully for me to do it, even though I knowed there was a chance I wouldn't be there too long. I warn't lying because that's how I felt the moment when I said it.

Ms. Douglas made me take a bath that night but I didn't mind as much because I kind of thought of myself like Carolina and tried to take some pleasure out of it, just like she did. And I got up real early the next morning, even before the sun come up, so I could help Miguel some more, so I warn't uncomfortable clean for too long. Some of the work was tough, like cleaning out the stable with all the mess that Carolina made or getting a heavy saddle up on her back or hauling a bale of hay from Miguel's truck. You might say that I was going against my normal inclination against doing *work*, but that's a word that gets used too often and covers too much ground, from real lowdown things that you'd never ever want to do all the way over to things that a body might take pleasure in under the right circumstantials.

You prob'ly think that things was going pretty good for me and that I'd feel pretty warm about it. But it warn't entirely the case. Every once in a while something or t'other would remember me of Pap and it seemed to kind of take the tuck all out of me every time.

One night I had a dream that shook me up considerable. I went down to the stable and I seen Miguel there but when I got up close it was Pap not Miguel. He was in one of his humors, and he was speaking Mexigrant but angry-like, not easy like Miguel. I tried to run but old Pap was too fast, like he always was, and pretty soon I found myself on the wrong end of a beating and a bad one. Carolina was making all kind of noise from inside on account of wanting to fend for me. And Pap got up offa me and says, "Somebody needs to shut that horse up." He warn't speaking Mexigrant no more. And then he made off in that direction and I sprung up fast and grabbed him, but then he turned and hit me so good in the head that I waked up sweating in my bed. I suppose I shoulda seen it as a sign of things to come, but instead I tried to go back to sleep even though it ain't easy to go back to sleeping after a dream like that.

But generally life with them ladies and Miguel was good and fine, 'cept that it lacked for the real proper kind of 'venture that would appeal to me or Tom Sawyer or Ben Rogers. I looked up Tom's number one night and tried to get him on the phone line, but his Aunt Polly answered the phone and she didn't believe me when I told her I was Tom's teacher, a-calling to check up on whether he done his scientific project yet. She told me that it warn't right to lie and warn't liable to get me what I was after. So I asked if she woulda let me talk to him if I'd just a said right off that it was Huckleberry Finn. And she says, "No, of course not." And so I 'splained to her that lying was clearly the better course of action, 'cause the lie at least had a chance of working out in my favor, whereas the truth was bound to fail. Well, she must have seen the logic in that—she was a lawyer after all—cause she said goodbye and hung up on the phone.

Even if it warn't the same as St. Petersburg, there was still lots of stuff to learn about in California. Everything was different than it was back home. At the grocery store, they had all these people standing around handing out food on little twigs, and I couldn't figger out why Miss Watson would still buy all sorts of stuff, seeing as a body could eat well enough just by going 'round and 'round and eating free stuff offa the twigs.

Every other afternoon Miss Watson would take me to the movies, which was one of my favorite things. I was always wanting to see the ones where there was a man or a woman with super powers which would help 'em fight bad guys. But after a time it got to feeling like I was watching the same one over and over, just with different colors. One fellow would wear black, and then another fellow would wear blue or green, and that's the only way you could tell the difference atwixt them. So Miss Watson took me to another kind of movie that was real sad and had lowdown people and nuthin never happened at all. Turns out there are just as many movies like that as the kind with super powers and bad guys. But they was all pretty much the same too. The kind of movie that I liked best was the kind that warn't the same all the time but always surprised you a little bit no matter how much you thought you knowed what might happen. A movie like that would always make you feel a little bit different at the end than you did at the beginning, most like you was changed in some kind of way, even though you might look exactly the same if you was to look in a mirror. Movies like that warn't very easy to find, but me and Miss Watson always hoped that every one would turn out like that. You prob'ly guessed that I'm the kind of person who would get all tingly at the beginning, when they turned the lights down low, and Miss Watson was that way too.

One day Miguel took me to the store to get stuff for Carolina and the other horses. It was a special store called a tack room where they had horseshoes and saddles and saddle pads and brushes and all such stuff as a horse could ever want. He got me my own special brush that I could use with Carolina, and it made me feel all warm inside, like she was my horse, even though nobody can really own a horse, 'cause a horse is her own owner, like Miguel learned me. But he also learned me that what you can do is care for 'em just like they was a member of your own family. That way, you belong to them as much as they belong to you.

He got me some real tasty ice cream, which was good because it was considerable hot that day. Just as we was finishing up with the sticky part of the cone where all the melty ice cream dribbles, a man all dressed up with shiny shoes come up to us and started conversating with Miguel.

He wanted to know if Miguel had a house of his own, and Miguel said no he didn't. Well, the man said it was his right to own a house, and Miguel he allowed that he wanted to have one some day. And the man he lit up with a big smile, as if he'd been waiting all day just to hear somebody say something as simple as that. He said that he was in the business of giving people money to buy a house. He said that he'd be happy to give Miguel near on a million dollar to buy whatever house he wanted.

Well Miguel he was mighty suspeptical. He told the man that he warn't quite ready to buy a house but that he was saving up as much as he could and he'd maybe come back when he was ready. He said it all political like, so the man wouldn't get mad and would maybe leave us to our ice cream. But the man said it didn't matter how much money Miguel had and that all he had to do was sign a few papers. He wanted us to come into his office with him. He kept mentioning that million dollar like it was just inside, tucked in a drawer or kept in a briefcase or something.

But Miguel was firm and strong. He said he warn't likely to be able to pay him back his million dollars, so he warn't interested. But the man said that ain't no matter 'cause it ain't his money exactly, so he didn't care whether Miguel paid it back or not. So then I jumped in and I asked him about the folks whose money it is. Wouldn't they be worried about getting paid back? And he said he reckoned prob'ly not, because the gov'ment would pay them back if Miguel didn't. He said the gov'ment was good that way, always trying to do a good turn for people.

But then I started wondering about the gov'ment, and so I said well what about the gov'ment then? Surely they'd want Miguel to pay it back. But no—he said it ain't really the gov'ment's money either, because they got it from regular folk just like Miguel, the taxpayers he called 'em. And I said well, then, prob'ly the taxpayers are gonna be upset if Miguel don't pay 'em back, and he said no again. He said that Miguel his own self is a taxpayer, and so it was just as if Miguel was loaning hisself a million dollars. He summed it all up by saying that it wouldn't be right for Miguel to turn down such a generous offer from hisself. If Miguel didn't like the house after a time, he could just give it back.

Well it was a powerful argument, and I thought maybe Miguel should give it a try. But Miguel said it was all malarkum. That's how it is with a Mexigrant sometimes. They don't see the sense of a thing even if it's staring at them right in the nose. Before we left the man started to see that the house thing didn't have a chance with Miguel, so he switched his angle. He said that the gov'ment was even more keen to give us money to go to college. And they didn't even care whether it was a real college or not, or whether we learned anything, or whether we finished what we started. The gov'ment just wanted us to get started and would give us all the money we wanted.

But Miguel didn't buy that one neither. He said he reckoned that he preferred work to school, especially if it was a school where you didn't have to learn anything but just had to pay near on a million dollar that the gov'ment had given you. After we walked away, he told me that the man would get some money hisself if he got us to take some, so we had to be careful. But to my way of thinking, Miguel was passing up a right solid opportunity. It was no wonder that people in California was so rich. They didn't need diamonds hanging from the sky, since there was men everywhere trying to hand out money and the gov'ment was behind them all the way.

CHAPTER 9

I Adjusticate to Living in California

NOW I woulda been mighty happy to stay up there and help Miguel most days and now and then take a day off to explore. But them ladies had another idea. They had an aim to sivilize me. I guess they thought they was doing me a good turn, but it didn't neither feel that way to me. Still some good come of it because I got to see things and try to understand this new place.

They took me to church which was most like a church in Missouri. My mama had taken me two or three time before she went away. Just like in Missouri the main activity of church in California was deciding when to stand and when to sit. Every time a body would get comfortable in a particular position, everybody else would make to change, and you'd have to follow them or else look silly on account you was doing something different. Of course they read from the Bible too, just like Missouri, but they most often left out all the good parts where folks was getting their heads chopped off or turned into stone.

The main difference from Missouri was that this

church that the ladies favored had a rock-and-roll band up on the stage right next to the preacher, prob'ly so that the people could pretend they warn't at church at all and was really at a concert instead. It was bully by me until I realized that the band was playing some kind of version that warn't so lowdown and mean as proper rock-and-roll.

The preacher he was pretty good and spent a lot of time telling us how we had to treat the Mexigrants right because they was people too just like the ones that was there. He was so friendly toward the Mexigrants I wondered why none of 'em had decided to come out to church that morning. Maybe they was still working or maybe they had their own church where the preacher was talking about how they had to treat regular folk right, on account of they warn't no worse than the Mexigrants.

Ms. Douglas she took me to school too. As I told you before, I'm none too keen on it. But she said that we didn't have no choice in the matter on account it was the law. At this school we went 'round and 'round the hallways, looking into the rooms with the headmaster. But mostly they was just quiet. The kids was filling in papers with little bubbles, and the teachers was generally just reading a book or maybe the newspaper at the front. The headmaster said that the kids at his school was particular good at filling in the right bubbles and not the wrong ones. He was monstrous proud I could tell, but I myself couldn't see what profit could come from filling in bubbles.

At the end, we went and set in a little room where there was a Mexigrant man and his daughter. Ms. Douglas and the Mexigrant man went in to talk to the headmaster, leaving me alone with the girl whose name was Ariel. Well she 'splained to me that she might not be able to get into the school because she lived on t'other side of a line that was drawn around the school that showed who would go to school there and who couldn't. She said that most of the folks who lived inside the line was regular white people, and most of the folks who lived outside was the Mexigrants. Well, as I said before, I ain't none too keen on school, but some folk have a real inclination for it. I don't hold no grudge against 'em just because they think something different than me. And Ariel was that way. I could tell that she wanted to go to this school real bad, maybe because she wanted to learn which bubbles to fill in. So I told her that—if it come to it—she could have my spot, since it didn't make no sense for me to take the place of a perfectly bully person who really wanted to be there.

When the door opened up, Ms. Douglas and the Mexigrant man, who was Ariel's father, come out again. And I could tell by the look on his face that he didn't get the answer that he wanted, and Ariel could tell right away too. She looked awful sad, and it most breaked my heart. The headmaster he wanted to talk to me in private, and he told me that the school would take me but I'd have to do some tutorial before I started, and Ms. Douglas and Miss Watson was gonna tutorial me. So I tried to 'splain it to him how it could all work out so that Ariel could go to school and I could be free of it, but he said it didn't work that way. He said that his school was a *public* school, and the wonderful thing about a public school is that it belongs to everybody in a way, including Ariel. And—since the school belongs to her—it warn't right for her to complain too much just 'cause she warn't allowed in there. It was better for her to be thankful that she could go to school at all. And he said the reason the gov'ment made the schools in the first place was to help children like Ariel get educated, and so it was Ariel's job to stay on her side of the line and go to the school that the gov'ment wanted her to, even if it warn't no good. And it was only jus' an *accident* that she and all the other Mexigrants was on the wrong side of the line. Well I turned it over in my brain a few time, but it still didn't make no sense to me. I ain't naturally inclined to stay anywheres that somebody tells me to, even if'n it is the gov'ment. But I suppose that the gov'ment knows best about a thing like that. I thought about Ariel then and wished and hoped that she'd find a good school or maybe she'd have a turn of thinking and come around to my position that book-learning is overappreciated.

Later that day Ms. Douglas took me to see her work, which was in one of the very top floors of one of them skyscratchers. It was monstrous tall, and the elevation closet made you feel like your insides was sloshing around. She 'splained to me that she was something called a management insultant. Far as I could tell, it meant that she didn't have to do work all day but instead spent all her time telling other people how to do their work or even speculating on how they might could do it better if they did something different. Well, I don't never want to work in a skyscratcher, but if I do, then I might could be a management insultant, like Ms. Douglas, since I'd ruther be the one telling other folks what to do than the other way

'round, though of course I prefer to be free and clear and everyone else too.

For a while Ms. Douglas had some meetings where she warn't allowed to bring me, so she told me to stay in these real nice chairs and read some magazines, but the only magazines they had was about business and other such subjects that a body'd never want to read about in a thousand year, so pretty soon I snuck off and found the elevation closet. I rode up and down for a time, just taking pleasure in that sloshing feeling of my insides. Lots of folks got in and out but they all pretended they warn't feeling anything, or maybe they done it too many times and it lost its special feeling for 'em. That's why I always like to be doing something different all the time. That way you don't lose any feelings but instead hang onto 'em for longer, especially the good ones.

After a while I reached up and pressed the very top button which was for the floor at the very top. I figgered that they'd have a real good view up there where I could see all of Los Angeles and maybe even the ocean. Well I got out and tried to go to the window, but there was a lady there, standing guard you might say, without which you wanted to be accurate, and then you'd say she was sitting guard. She was just about the prettiest sight you'd ever seen, and she smiled so that you felt like you was just who she'd been waiting to see all day long. But then it turned out that she warn't so welcoming after all—her smile was a kind of a show—and she told me that I had to go back down where I come from and that they didn't want me there. Well it didn't seem fair that she would try to speak for all the folk there. Maybe there was somebody who wanted to meet me but didn't know it yet.

I made to go back to the elevation closet, but instead I got real small like a muskrat or a possum. I got down on the floor and crawled all the way past her. That's what happens when you set at a desk for too long—it makes it so you can't see stuff that's right in front of your eyes. I stayed real low and real flat and real close to the desk and went right past her feet. They was the prettiest feet a body'd ever seen. I'd say that her feet was prettier even than a lot of people's faces, and generally it's the face that's more pretty than the rest. But I didn't stop too long to admire 'em. I just kept going 'cause I was decided to get past her and see the ocean and maybe make some discoveries too.

Well I walked 'round and 'round. That's how it was up there—a big circular. And all around the inside was lots of women with pretty feet sitting up real straight so as they could see far. And all around the outside was big rooms with big windows. And there was men in there mostly, sitting on couches or ottermans or maybe typing at something important. Nobody payed no tension to me at all. That's how it is in California. If you act like you got a right to be there, then everybody thinks it's so. It don't matter how you look or what kind of clothes you wear. But you gotta get yourself to believe it first, and sometime that's the hardest part.

Well I had to uricate so I followed some fellow out of his office and down to the laboratory where there was real pretty stone fountains wherein you could take a leaker. So I did and I noticed that there was a blinking light on the fountain, most like it was a car that wanted to make a turn. I waited a while and kept a close look on it, but it didn't go nowheres.

The sink was most magic like and sprayed water whenever you went near it, and then stopped when you went away. Ben Rogers woulda said that maybe Old Mrs. Loftus had something to do with it. But just 'cause a thing seems like magic don't mean that it is magic. The way I figgered it, there was prob'ly a man behind the mirror. I was thinking of the one I'd seen in a policecop show one time, the kind of mirror that you can see through from the other side. And so there was a man back there who was watching real close every time I come up to the sink, and he's the one would turn the water off and on real quick. I waved real hard and smiled too, because it seemed like it'd be a dreadful lonesome job, but he didn't give no sign that he seen me. Maybe that was against the rules.

That other man—the one that warn't hiding behind a mirror, but the one I followed into the laboratory—he was still there, and he kept looking at me funny, even though he was done washing his hands. And finally he collected up his courage to say something.

"What's up, kid?"

Well it warn't a proper question so I didn't give him a proper answer neither. I just shruggled my shoulders and walked past him. But he must've got it in his brain that I warn't meant to be there, because he followed me right out the door and kept asking questions that I warn't in-clined to answer. Finally he asked just how I got in there, and I told him that I snuck by the lady with the pretty

feet. Sometime the truth don't hurt none, more often than
a body would think. And that's how it was this time. He
thought I was right clever to do it, even though I told him
that it hardly took a thought.

"Come back to my office, Huckleberry." I'm not saying that he guessed my name right off. I had told it to
him by that particular time. He said that I showed a lot
of gumpshun and that I was just like him or he was just
like me, I couldn't tell straight on. I followed him back
down to the biggest office you ever seen. It was right on
the end, where there was a turn in the circular. And there
was windows so big that there warn't any wall left around
the outside. This fellow showed me the ocean way far off
in the distance, and he said that it was too far to see the
pirates or the giant squids or anything else. But they was
there whether we could see 'em or not.

Now this man—he called hisself the President but not
the President like you think. He said he was the top man
at his company and all the other people had to do what he
told them to do. But he said he tried to do it nice and easy,
so as they wouldn't get sore at him. He seemed to think
that I was angling for his job, and he kept telling me how
I might be a President one day just like him. Well, I was
suspeptical that I would be comfortable in a situation like
that, but I didn't see no profit in telling him so.

I told him that I was adjusticating best I could to life
in California, but he was pretty keen on telling me that
it was better if I went all the way to the other side of the
country. He said that it was more bully over there. In California, you would judge a man's quality by the kind of

car he might drive or if he looked like a movie star. But that was superficious, he said. It was much better to judge a man by which type of school he went to or whether his mom and dad had lots of money in the bank and a big, big house. It was more accurate that way. And that's where he'd come from, he said, and that's how it came that he was smarter than all these folks in California and how he'd risen up to be the top man. Well, I didn't tell the man, but I didn't have much interest in going to school or living in a big house. But I guess I didn't want a fancy car neither, and nobody'd never mistooken me for a movie star. So I couldn't rely on anyone to have a high 'pinion of me, on neither side of the country. But it warn't no matter to me what they thought.

The President wanted to teach me all about his business. He was monstrous proud and wanted me to tell him how bully everything was. So I did. His business was making medicines, and he said that they made so much money they didn't know where to put it no more. He 'troduced me to one fellow who was in charge of making pretty TV shows that would get people to take more medicine. The President said that this fellow was particular good at learning people they was sick, because there was all sorts of people who didn't know they was sick until they watched one of them shows.

Another fellow was only in charge of making sure that the gov'ment didn't decide that their medicine was bad or illegal. I told 'em not to worry, that I knowed there was folks who made good profits even after the gov'ment decided that the medicine they was selling was illegal. I told them all about Jefe, and I meant it to make 'em feel good but they didn't 'ppreciate the comparable. Last the President 'troduced me to a woman there who he said was the smartest of 'em all, and she was in charge of counting all the money and hiding it from the gov'ment.

By this time, we had walked all the way back to the front, where the lady with the pretty feet was sitting. And you shoulda seen her 'spression when she seen me with the President. She was just about to be mean and low-down to me when she seen that he was treating me with 'spectability. So she got real nice all of a sudden and even offered to give me some water. The President he was still keen on me and wanted me to come work for him for free, kind of like a slave, but he called it an intern. Well some people might be happy to be slaves or interns, but not me. So I left him there, and the lady with the pretty feet was awful pleased to see me go.

CHAPTER 10

Me and Miguel
Make a Rescue

IT was a kind of adventuring to meet all those fancy people and to do all those city things. You wouldn't think so but it remembered me of what me and Ben Rogers used to do down by the big river, when we'd just go wandering and see what we could find and what people we could meet. And I made up my brain that the city warn't quite so different as people back home might 'magine it to be.

But it didn't neither mean that I gave up on adventuring out in the wild. Sometime you hear that big cities ain't got no critters but just people and rats. Los Angeles ain't that way at all. And Miguel he had a way with the critters, even the wild ones. He knowed all the names of the birds and what they'd eat and where they'd prefer to make their nest. One night, just as the sun was going down behind the mountain, he took me out to a hill where we could look out into some trees and he showed me a nest. It was a raven's nest, and I hadn't never seen one before. It was a monstrous proud bird, and Miguel said that sometime they'd even chase a hawk or an eagle, if they didn't want 'em around. Miguel said they was one of the smartest birds too and could learn to talk a few words, if you had one as a pet. There was three chicks in the nest that we could see. They was gray and fuzzy, most like baby rabbits, and not black like a proper raven that was full grown. Miguel he brought some bifoculars so as we could see 'em from far away.

At first it was just the baby chicks in the nest, but then the mama raven swooped in and come to feed 'em. They was squawking and squirming, all trying to get in the best position to be fed. And their mouths was open as wide as they could go. Miguel and me traded turns with the bifoculars, so we could both see. The mama raven stuck her beak into each one of their mouths, and Miguel said that she was sharing food that she'd already gotten for herself. You'da thunk that it might be disgustable to see such a thing, but it warn't at all. It seemed like the way it oughta be, and them chicks was mighty thanksful for all they got. When she was done, she flew off to go find more food, on account all her babies was still hungry.

Well, we was getting ready to go back to the house when I heard something down below. I looked down there and I seen it right away. It was a coon that was climbing the tree. And me and Miguel knowed right away that he had heard all the squawking and had come to see if maybe the raven babies would make for a good supper. And right behind him was two other coons a-following the first. And now we knowed that the raven babies was in a tough spot, 'cause their mama had flown off far away and warn't there to protect them no more. Miguel made to yell and clap

so as to scare the coons off. They looked up to see what the kermotion was, but we warn't close enough to make 'em fully afeard. So then they kept going up the tree. Well it most breaked my heart to know that those babies was gonna make for a coon supper. And Miguel was broken up about it too. So he told me to stay there and run off back to the house. Pretty soon he come back with a gun. He got there just in time too, 'cause they was coming up on the nest which was near the top of the tree.

Miguel he fired the gun a couple of time up in the air. And the coons looked up at us again like they was curious what the noise was, but they didn't look afeard at all. So Miguel brought the gun down and aimed it at the tree.

"I'm not going to shoot them, *muchacho*," says Miguel. "I just want to scare them off."

CRACK! He took a shot. And this time it worked. The bullet musta hit one of the smaller branches, 'cause there was a crash of leaves. Two of the coons got spooked and went running down the trunk of the tree and didn't neither look back to see what it was. The other one, though, lost his footgrip and slipped off his branch. He hit a couple of bigger branches as he was falling and then landed on the ground which was full of rocks. It was a long way. I didn't want to see him eat those raven babies, but I didn't neither want to see him take a fall like that. Miguel scrambled down the hill to check on him, and I followed him close. But we both knowed that he warn't gonna survive a fall like that. And we was right. The fall had killed him dead. Miguel didn't feel good about it, but I told him it was just an accident and not his fault at all. So we made a hole in the ground for him and left him in there. It made us sad, but there warn't no other way.

Well we thought it was finished then, but a couple of days later Ms. Douglas said that the cats were all shook up about something. Me and Miguel went out and found 'em prowling around a cactus type plant that was out near the front driveway. The leaves was long and prickly, only a lot of 'em was dead and brown. The cats—Ms. Douglas had a couple of 'em that warn't proper pets but lived outside most like they was wild bobcats—they was circling around this plant and making a ruckus. Pretty soon we figgered out that there was some kind of animal up in there, and the cats was all excited to get at it and play with it and maybe eat it too. Miguel he shooed them cats away, and we got up close to see. Well it was too tight for Miguel, so he sent me in, and that's when I found 'em. There was a little space in there, under the dead part of the plant, and there was six baby coons in there, as cute as could be. Miguel said he was sure that they was the babies of the one that had died, so it must've been a her 'stead of a him. And they was a-gonna make for cat food if we didn't save 'em. So he gave me a shoebox with some old rags in it and sent me back under the bush.

"Be careful, *muchacho*," Miguel says. "Make sure you get all of them." He said that it warn't their fault that their mama was a-gonna eat the raven babies, and anyway that was just the way of things out in the woods. Still, they was small, and it was our job to take care of 'em best we could.

Well I did and we brought them back to the house. Miss Watson made up a potion of milk and eggs, and she let me feed 'em with an eye dropper that was made for people. Ms. Douglas got on the phone with some kind of place that would take good care of 'em until they was old enough to go out into the wild. We only kept 'em that one night but it was one of my favorite nights. Saving baby coons ain't something I ever done even back in St. Petersburg, and I got Miguel to thank for it. We still felt bad about the mama, but maybe a little less, 'cause we was able to save her babies. It was even sad to say goodbye to 'em but I knowed that coons warn't made to be pets and live in a house. They'd be happiest out in the woods, just like me.

After that I got to pretending that I was a coon, and I'd go exploring outside. Usually it was during the day, but sometime I'd find a way to get out after Ms. Douglas and Miss Watson had gone to bed. There was that tree outside my window, you remember. Well one night I was out exploring the hill and I come by the little creek that run through the woods back there. It was just a trickle most of the time but would turn into more of a proper creek after there'd been rain. Well I knowed from back home that a creek was bound to turn into a stream and that a stream was bound to turn into a bigger stream and so on until you come to a river.

So I made my way down following the trickle of the water. It was the end of a hot day—though we never had hot days like that in the winter back in Missouri. The winter was different in California, not like a proper winter at all. The creek kept it cool like, though, and there was lots of tree cover to make it shadowy and shady, which made a body feel right at home.

Well I was right of course, and the little creek got bigger, little by little, and pretty soon I come to a pipe in the ground where the creek emptied into. I got down real low and peered down there. It was dark and bubbly down there, so much so that it most gave me the fantods. I knowed that it just went down to the river, but I 'magined that it led to a different place altogether, a place where there was magical things and strange people and critters of all different kinds that a body'd never seen before. It felt like that pipe was maybe something out of a storybook. I had an inclination to go down in there, spite of my fantods, but the time warn't right yet, I suppose. And somehow it turned out that my 'magination was closer on to the truth than I ever woulda thunk back then. But I'm a-getting to that part.

CHAPTER 11

Gallivanting
with the Grangerfords

THERE'S one other thing I want to tell about before I tell what happened to me and Miguel on the river. There was some high-class folks that lived up over the hill from Ms. Douglas and Miss Watson. This family they called they-selves the Grangerfords and they was of a higher class than Ms. Douglas or even the Judge. They was out looking for their dog who had run away, and the boy—his name was Buck—he asked for my help. So Miss Watson and me rode all over further than we had originally 'tended to go, on account of we could cover more territory than they could go on foot. And 'ventually we did find the dog, a tiny little yapper dog, and brung it back to Buck and his sisters, and they made a big hoo-ha about it and invited me to come visit them on the house up on the hill.

Well Ms. Douglas she dropped me off up there. It was a bigger house than you ever seen before, and there was a monstrous thick wall all the way 'round it. Outside the gate was all sort of folk with cameras that warn't allowed through the gate but stayed outside all day waiting to chase them Grangerfords down and take their photograms all the time. On the inside was all such stuff as high-class people have, like butlers and maids and a statue of a whale right when you come in the front door. There was more folks with cameras inside the house too, only these ones was allowed to be there by the family, and would follow every one of 'em around everywhere they went 'cept the bathroom, without which there was some kind of fight or argument going on and then they'd go in the bathroom too, so as not to miss any of the retorts.

Now Buck he 'splained to me that his sisters was real high-class. The reason they was so high-class was that Buck's mama had been on a TV show all about rich and famous people for near on a year, and Buck's father had one time been one of them football players. The cameras was there for a TV show that was all about the Grangerfords and that showed most everything about them. They called it *Gallivanting with the Grangerfords*, and everybody was monstrous proud of how many million people watched every week.

Every one of 'em had the biggest kind of dreams a body had ever heard of. Buck he wanted to be a movie star just like his mama, and his sister Miss Lilian wanted to be a singer that would wear a swimsuit at night and dance so good that everybody in the world would want to be like her. She did a show for us and I didn't see too much profit in dancing like that, but that's prob'ly on account that I warn't raised to be high-class. And there was Miss Sophia, who dreamed about being a famous photogrammer though I only ever saw her taking pictures of herself, and Miss Charlotte who warn't yet decided how she was gonna stay famous but was certain that there was profit in it.

I figgered if maybe I hung 'round with them Grangerfords for a while that I'd get the hang of it and maybe be a little bit more high-class than I started. But it was hard getting around in that house from one room to the next, 'cause you'd always run into one of Buck's sisters and she'd have eleven or so people following with cameras and mikerphones and such equipparatus as you need to take a video picture, and you'd most get stampeded and then have to retreat real fast and go back the way you come until you find a doorway to duck into. I most got stampeded every time.

Well Buck took a hankering to me, on account he was surrounded by so many females trying to make theyselves more and more famous, which can be an awful tedious way to disseminate your days. So he got to inviting me to come along whenever the family would go out. Most times we'd go to the shopper mall so the sisters could try out different kinds of clothes and buy such stuff that would make their mama and papa spiteful and angrified. Now they was nice girls, mostly, so 'ccassionally a man would have to step in and tell 'em what to fight about, so there'd be something for everybody to care about on the television show. He called hisself the Producer. And those girls did a bully job of fighting good. Mostly it was with words and bad faces but then every once in a while they'd take to hitting or slapping each other, and it was an awful good show. Everybody in the world was interested in what kind of trouble they'd get into or what kind of things they'd fight about, prob'ly so's they could learn what kind of trouble and fights was high-class, ruther than low-class.

CHAPTER 12

A Scandalous Marriage Proposition

ONE day with the Grangerfords was more bully than the rest though. They took me down to the beach which I'd been itching to see ever since I come to California.

It warn't nuthin like I was 'specting. There was some palm trees like Pap said, but there was more people than trees. And the people was of all different types and had the strangest hair you ever seen, most like they was a peacock or a zebra or a little bit of both. It didn't smell nuthin like Missouri or even the Salton Sea. It was its own special smell, but it was mixed in with a funny kind of smell that remembered me of Mrs. Loftus back in St. Petersburg. You'd never think but the beach in Los Angeles is like a circus, only better 'cause you don't gotta pay nuthin to get in. There was a whole group of people who had wheels on their shoes and real frilly costumes and they was dancing and rolling around like they was birds or maybe fish in the sea. There was a man who had a saber that he stuffed down his throat most like it was a piece of food. The saber was so long that Buck and me thought maybe it would come right out of his stomach, but it never did. After he took the saber back out of his mouth, everybody cheered to see that he warn't dead, and then he come 'round with a tin can and everybody pulled out their wallets and purses and gave him all such money as they had, prob'ly as payment so as he wouldn't try it again. Then there was a woman who was most covered in snakes, even with one big yellow 'un wrapped around her neck on account it was hoping to eat her for lunch. Well it most gave me the fantods to see it, but it was monstrous bully too. Those snakes was so big they must've come from the jungle or somewheres real far from Missouri or even California. After the snakes, Buck and I went to check out a kermotion up on a little hill, and there was hunderts of people dancing around while some other people played drums. Buck and me pretended that we was wild Injuns and danced as hard as we could, and everybody clapped and told us how bully we was.

There was so much entertainment that everybody was forgetting that they was at the beach, so nobody was in the water but just up on the sidewalk watching the circus. But Buck and me got free of his sisters and we went into the water. We was hot then because of all the dancing. It most remembered me of the big river back home, but it was different too, on account that China was on the other side. We looked hard and thought maybe we saw it one or two time. There warn't no pirates that I could see, but I guessed that maybe they only come out at night. I couldn't rightly 'splain the lack of giant whales or squid. But Buck said that they was under the water, and we had to be careful not to step on a tentacle or else be pulled into the ocean and eaten for a squid snack.

Well, pretty soon we heard a kermotion up on the sand, so we come running out to find out that Buck's sister Miss Sophia had gone missing, spite all of the camera people and the Producer and her sisters. It was an awful ruckus, all those girls screaming for their sister and the Producer trying to get the camera folk to listen to him and get it all down on video picture. Everybody had a 'pinion. Buck thought that maybe she drowned or got eaten by a squid, but Miss Lilian said that she was kidnapped by low-class folks who prob'ly wanted a ransom and they'd all end up in the poor house and not be on TV anymore. But the Producer—he was kind—he told 'em that it'd be bully by him if they was poor and he wouldn't take 'em off TV. Well that had a beneficial impact on everyone's psychometry, so they started to make a plan to find Miss Sophia, dead or alive, and maybe get revenge on those people who had kidnapped her. And that's when Lilian got a message on her phone, and we all's heard her yelp when she looked at it. Well it was a video picture of Miss Sophia, and she was with a boy I'd never seen before. They was hugging each other and crying, and Miss Sophia told how she had fallen in love with Harney Shepherdson. I didn't know who that was, but everybody else did, so Buck 'splained to me that Harney Shepherdson was one of the Shepherdson clan who was much lower class than the Grangerfords. They had their own television show on a different channel—they called it *Schmoozing with the Shepherdsons*—only it didn't get as many million people to watch it, and the people who did watch it was much lower class than the folk who watched the Grangerfords.

If you thought that there was a ruckus before, then I don't know what you would call what happened next on the beach. Everybody was crying and yelling and was even more upset, on account of Miss Sophia warn't just dead or kidnapped but was associating with the lowest kind of folk on television. In the kermotion, Miss Lilian dropped her phone into the sand, I seen her do it myself. And the Producer swooped in to pick it up and look at the video picture again. Pretty soon he had everybody's tension and was saying that he knowed where Miss Sophia was on account of some hidden clues in the video picture. We went up the street a bit—the whole swarm of us—and found a restaurant that had all sort of stuff about pirates, not real pirates but fake 'uns. Still they had some bully sabers and guns and a talking parrot in one corner, but all he'd say was "Ahoy me hearties" and only then when the fellow would give him a piece of popcorn. It warn't how a real pirate would talk but it was bully by me, 'cause I'd never seen a bird that could talk pirate before. So fake pirate was good enough for me.

But I'm a-letting the story meamble away from me. Buck and me only had five minute or so to talk to the parrot before that Producer fellow found Miss Sophia. She was up on the second floor of the restaurant with Harney Shepherdson only they warn't alone. They was there with a whole army of Shepherdsons crowded 'round them. The Producer pointed everybody where to go, and Buck and me was sure we was gonna see a real war. Buck he wanted to get in there too, on account he had high-class Granger-ford blood, but I was inclined to take a more observational view and hold my low-class blood in reserve, so I removed myself over to the wall where I clumb up on a table so as I could see how the matter would play itself out. Well there was pushing and pulling, and people was yelling bad names hither and forth. The Shepherdsons warn't just the Shepherdsons but also their folks with the cameras and the mikerphones and everything else. Pretty soon Miss Sophia and Harney Shepherdson was catched in the middle of it all, and everybody was pulling on them from both the Grangerford and the Shepherdson sides, so they got up on the table and before you knowed it they was climbing up in the rafters above us while all their families tried to pull 'em back down.

Now Harney finally got real mad and he yelled so loud it made most everybody shut up right away. He said that he was in love with Miss Sophia and he didn't care that she was a Grangerford. Now the Grangerfords made a big ruckus, but he started yelling again and pretty soon they quiet down. He was gonna love her to the very end of his life, even if it meant that he couldn't be a Shepherdson no more. And now the Shepherdsons all chimed in with their yelling and screaming until Harney done something that got everyone to go all still and quiet like there was a funeral. He got down on his knees and asked Miss Sophia to marry him. You think I'm telling you a stretcher, but I'm not. That's exactly what he done. It was hard for him up in the rafters to go down on his knees but somehow he managed it and had to look up at her after he done it. Well she was smiling big and pretty, and it didn't take her no time to say yes and then they got to kissing and fell out of the rafters and was taken up by the angry mob, and suddenly there warn't no difference atwixt Grangerford and Shepherdson. They was all mad at Miss Sophia and Harney. It looked to me like a full on riot was coming on.

But I seen that the Producer was kind of off to the side, talking quietly with this other woman who was there from the Shepherdson side. And they was shaking hands. Pretty soon they went 'round and told all the camera folks to put away their cameras and the mikerphones too. And after a while the riot started to come down a bit as the participants realized that there warn't no cameras on no more. And when it got quiet enough the Producer and the other woman walked into the middle and pulled Miss Sophia and Harney off of the floor. They was a little scratched up but they come out okay. Now the Producer he got everybody's tension and said that there was a real good solution to this whole thing and that it was that they would do a big TV show with the wedding. Well a few people cheered then, who thought that was satisfactual.

And he said the wedding would be on the Grangerford channel, and then there was booing and cussing from the Shepherdson side. But then the woman spoke up—you prob'ly already guessed that she was the Producer for the Shepherdson show—she said it would only be fair if the Shepherdson's channel got to show when Miss Sophia and Harney had a fight and breaked up for good. Well there was more cheers then, only it still depended on Miss Sophia and Harney. They was whispering to theyselves for a minute, but pretty soon Harney come out and said that they was all for it, and that they'd already had some disagreeables that would make for a real good fight for to break 'em up and it wouldn't neither take very long after the wedding. Well there was cheers all 'round then and from both sides, and pretty soon the cameras and mikerphones was back on and everybody was having a party most like they was planning to do it all along anyway.

CHAPTER 13

Trouble Comes Hunting

WELL before I knowed it weeks run along and I was most getting accustomated to that big bed and omelets every morning. Miss Watson took to teaching me proper spelling. I told her that it warn't for me, but she said I was intelligenic and that I'd be able to start school if I worked hard to catch myself up. But that just showed that she didn't understand my motorvation at all. I kept at it good enough I suppose, but just enough so she'd let me alone for the rest of the day.

Ms. Douglas was better. She had an inclination to 'venture and explore, and there was the woods just out back. They warn't proper woods, like back home, but they was bully just the same. There was the little creek running through there, as I told about before. Ms. Douglas let me run loose and even climb up on one of the big rocks that was at the top of the mountain. If you looked one way, there was hills as far as a body could see. And if you looked t'other way, there was the city out there down below, a-buzzing and a-bustling.

One day I clumb down and I seen something papery on the ground, and I knowed right away what it was. A snakeskin. I took it down to Ms. Douglas—she was resting in her usual spot down by the creek.

"Look what I found," I says. "It's a rattlesnake, isn't it?"

"I think you're right, Huckleberry." She had made a common habit out of calling me my whole proper name and not just Huck. "They're very dangerous. We lost one of our dogs two summers ago."

"He got bit?"

"She got bit. It was a baby. Their venom is the most potent."

She gave me an apple that was green and sour and delicious. We was quiet for a time then, and I knowed that she and I was okay together, like me and the Judge. We listened to the dribble-drabble of the creek and it was awful peaceable. It got me a-wondering.

"Where does this water come from?" I ask her.

"Well it comes from the top of the mountain. Some of it probably started as snow and some as rain."

"And it goes all the way to the ocean?"

"That's right."

"So if I was to drop a message into a bottle and leave it to the river, it could make it all the way down to Tom Sawyer?"

She thought about it a minute or two. "Maybe it would. As long as it didn't get caught up in the weeds or the rocks. There'd have to be a good rain, so the water would carry it all the way," she says. "But Tom would have to be there to catch it too, so it wouldn't go right off into the ocean. You wouldn't want your message to fall into the hands of some pirates, would you?"

Well it seemed like a long shot, and I didn't know what I'd say in a note to Tom anyway, 'specially since it'd probably be a few days before he'd get it. But I kept that idea in my brain, in case it might come useable some day.

I'd been thinking on it for some time, so I finally asked her my other question.

"Ms. Douglas," I says. "I was wondering if you was a thespian."

"What, a thespian? What do you mean?"

"Well my Pap says that a lady who marries a lady is a thespian."

She smiled a little bit then, like she understood what I was driving at. "Why, yes, Huckleberry. Why then I suppose I am a thespian."

"My Pap says it ain't right, a lady marrying a lady."

"And what about you? What do you think?"

I thought for a minute. I warn't necessarily advercating for Pap in the matter.

"I reckon it's like smoking," I says after I hit on it.

"Like smoking? In what way?"

"People get down on a thing when they don't know nuthin about it."

I don't know why, but that made her laugh a little bit. That's how it is in California. They laugh sometime when you're not making a joke, and they won't laugh some other time when you make a monstrous funny one.

"I've never thought about it that way, but I suppose maybe it is just a little bit like smoking."

She was quiet then and she looked out at the sky, where there was monstrous dark clouds overlooming the mountains.

"We need the rain," she says.

When we got back I went right to the stable to help Miguel with the horses. My main job was to groom Carolina, which she loved. First there was a special tool that you can use to pick all the dirt out of her hooves. And then you'd brush her, first with a hard brush that would get all the dirt and mud off of her body and then with a soft brush that would make her hide look all shiny and clean. The brushing made her feel good I could tell, and it remembered me of when my mama would scratch and rub my back. It was so long ago she went away that I couldn't recollect all the particulars but only just the feeling, which was awful warm and comfortable.

But it was different for Carolina on that day. She most had the fantods on account of the storm brewing up over our heads, so she warn't moving her head and making noises like normal, which was how she'd tell me that she liked what I was doing. I tried my best to make her more comfortable and less afeard but it warn't easy that day.

"Mansita, Carolina. Esta bien." I didn't say it as good as Miguel, but she understood what I was driving at and it helped settle her down considerable.

"She loves you, *muchacho*. I can tell." That was Miguel. He was working at a table, oiling Miss Watson's saddle. It was him that learned me how to take care of Carolina and brush her and make her feel comfortable. I ain't ashamed to say that I learned all that from a Mexigrant, 'cause he was awful 'sperienced and had a way of making a horse—or even a person—feel good about theyselves and their situation.

I was excited to show him my find, so I put Carolina back in her stable, and I pulled out the snakeskin and held it out to show Miguel. But he warn't happy like I thought he'd be.

"*¡Muchacho! ¡¿Que haces con eso?!*" Miguel he took a step backwards. "What are you doing with that?"

"It's a snakeskin," I says. "I found it out by the creek. Ms. Douglas says it jus' about the biggest one she's ever seen 'round here."

"She doesn't know, Huck. It's bad luck to touch a snakeskin with your hand."

"No it ain't."

"Yes it is. Where I come from, everybody knows it."

Well I put it away then. I didn't mean to cause a kermotion. But Miguel warn't done yet.

"It's a sign, *muchacho*. A sign of something bad to come. I feel it." Both Carolina and Miguel had got theyselves spooked good. He looked up at them clouds now, and they was even darker than before. It was most blue-black outside, and lovely, but Miguel couldn't see nuthin good at that particular time, only bad signs and such.

"It's not just that," he says. "Last night I saw a white owl. *Una lechusa.* A witch."

"That ain't nuthin," I told him. "We got owls like that back home."

"No, not like this, Huck. In my country, we say, *Cuando el tecolote canta, el indio muere.*"

"What does it mean?"

"The owl brings the death." Well I warn't afeard before, but Miguel had spooked me good by the end. That's
how it is most times. You can forget all the bad stuff for a
while and maybe think that you're done with it once and
for good. But pretty soon it comes creeping back in, even
if it's jus' in your brain.

Miguel had warned me good, but I got myself un-
spooked by the nighttime. I was laying in bed, listening to
the rain on the roof and it was an awful clatter. It rained
like all fury too, and begun to thunder and lightning. It remembered me of the summer storms back home in Missouri, though it warn't the summer in Los Angeles then.
Back home, me and Ben would head out and see what we
could find. It's just about the best time to be exploring, the
nighttime when it's a-raining. The world feels different at
a time like that. So you know what I did. I went out the
window via my usual method and I slithered down the
trunk of the oak tree which was wet with the rain. Well
by the end of the night I wished that I never had done it.

It was a mighty bully rainstorm, and I went up onto
the mountain. The trails was all slippery and I was able to
make an awful splash every time I brung my feet down. I
stood on top of the rock and looked down on Los Angeles,
and it seemed like the whole city was under the clouds and
was enjoying the effects of the rain. People said that it don't
rain in Los Angeles, but you don't have to believe 'em. I
seen it myself. Rain is good for a place. It washes things out,
like Pap and me did with the camper that one time, so that
everything feels clean and shiny and new in the morning.

I found a spot where there was a big rush of water a-coming off the mountain, so I rode it right down and landed soft and wet in the creek. It was so much fun I let off a shriek when I come down. So I clumb back up and did it near four or five time. There was mud all over me, and I was even a-shivering a bit, but fun like that has a way of making a body forget that he's a-shivering. I got to thinking about Tom Sawyer and wondering what he was doing in the middle of all this rain. If it was true about the river, then all this water that was falling on me would trickle and dribble all the way down to Tom. I hoped in my heart that there was a tree branch near his window and that he was able to escape down to the river to watch all the water wash down to the ocean. Maybe he was out there just now, standing 'neath the rain and wondering 'bout me.

When I had tuckered myself out, I headed back. There was a big thunderboom just as I was a-coming out of the woods, and I heard a ruckus out in the stable. Carolina was jumping and bucking like she warn't none too happy. I hunted around but there warn't no sign of Miguel, even though his apartment door was open and the light was on. I stole a sugar cube from the bowl on his table, and I went back to Carolina. Well she wouldn't take it from me directly, but I set it down where she could see it and I ducked out of her sight. She quieted down then and pretty soon I seen her slurp it up with her tongue. And she stayed quiet, so I knowed that it had done the trick and helped her get more comfortable.

I figgered I'd done my job for the night and was even feeling a little bit wore out, like I was ready to sleep. So

I went back to the oak tree and clumb up, which was always harder than coming down, but I could manage it pretty good now on account of a rain barrel that was next to the house.

I had clumb in the window and had a good feeling like you always do when you come back into your warm room after playing in the rain. I was standing over near my dresser and was taking off my muddy shirt when I heard it.

"You think you're a good deal of a big-bug, don't you?"

Well, the voice come from behind me, but I knowed right away that it was Pap. Somehow he found me. Like I told you before, he was smart. And I could tell you that I warn't afeard, but that wouldn't be the full true story.

"Maybe I am, maybe I ain't," I says. And I didn't neither turn around to look at him till I was done putting on a dry shirt. With a man like Pap, it's not always good to show him what you're a-feeling on the insides.

He was most fifty, and he looked it. He'd gone through an awful change since I seen him last. His hair was long and tangled and greasy, and hung down, and you could see his eyes shining through like he was behind vines. It was all black, no gray; so was his long, mixed-up whiskers. There warn't no color in his face. Where his face showed, it was white—not like another man's white, but a white to make a body sick, a white to make a body's flesh crawl, a tree-toad white, a fish-belly white. As for his clothes, they was just rags, that was all. He set there a-looking at me, leaning back in the chair.

"Don't you give me none o' your lip," says he. "You've

put on considerable many frills since I been away. I'll take you down a peg before I get done with you." He picked up my spelling book from the table right next to him.

"You learnin' to read and write?" Well I didn't answer.

"You think you're better'n your father, now, don't you, since he can't?"

"No sir."

"Who told you you might meddle with such hifalut'n foolishness, hey? Who told you you could?"

"Ms. Douglas did."

"Ms. Douglas, hey? And who told Ms. Douglas she could put in her shovel about a thing that ain't none of her business?"

"Nobody never told her."

"Well, I reckon I learnt her how to meddle."

That's when I seen the blood. It was dripping down Pap's sleeve, and it was making a little pool on the floor. And I knowed right then that this warn't the old Pap who was mostly bad but sometime good. I thought about Ms. Douglas then, and Miss Watson too.

"I understand you're rich. Got a big reward."

"I ain't got no money."

"That's a lie. That Judge has got it, don't he? You git it, I want it."

I took a step toward the door. There was a splinter of light coming in from the hallway.

"I told you, I ain't got no money."

Well Pap picked something up from the table. It was hid behind the book, so I hadn't seen it before. It was a knife and a big one too.

"It ain't right. That money's mine. You're my son. I had all the trouble and all the anxiety and all the expense of raisin' you, didn't I?"

Pap stood up.

"I ain't got no money," says I. And I was eyeing the door and hoping that Pap had hit the bottle that night and maybe wouldn't be quick like his normal self.

"What kind of a son are you?"

It warn't a question that begged for an answer, so I made a jump for the door. But Pap was too quick. He grabbed me from behind. I lunged for it and was able to get my head through the door and out into the light.

"Ms. Douglas! MS. DOUGLAS!" I screamed. I pulled as hard as I could, but Pap had a vicegrip on my arm and he pulled me back into the dark room. But I warn't done yet. I pulled with all my might and I come back out into the light. But he come with me and still had me by the arm. I seen his face in the light then and it had the look of the rabies, just like I thought. It happened all quick, first one thing then another and then another. But for me and Pap it seemed real slow, like time was getting pulled and stretched, on account we was in a battle atwixt our lives.

Well he was strong, and he got holt of my hair, and he held the knife right up to my neck like to slit my throat. "You ain't no son of mine no more," he says. I was pretty much done for and it was my own blood who was gonna do it. But just then—BAM! A big shadow come in and collisioned with Pap's nose. And I fell down to the ground, free and clear of Pap. It was Miguel. I never seen him in the house before, but here he was just when a body needed him most. Pap took it pretty bad, but the rabies was strong in him, so he got up most right away and went after Miguel with the knife. He didn't make no more words then but just a scream to make a body turn white like a ghost. But Miguel was too quick and he knocked the knife out of Pap's hands and it went over the railing and clanged down on the ground below.

I ran down the stairs to get the knife, thinking maybe I could help Miguel. But I was halfway down and I seen that Miguel had Pap beat. Pap got in a couple hard hits to Miguel, but Miguel he was strong and before you knowed it he had Pap cornered 'gainst the wall. I seen Pap's eyes fill up with the rabies again, and he rose hisself up. He picked up an awful heavy vase that was there in the hallway, and he come at Miguel with the vase held up high over his head. But it was a desperation move and Miguel he was quick. He stepped out of the way and even gave Pap a little shove and Pap toppled right over the railing and for a minute he was flying through the air like a raven, only with his arms flapping 'stead of wings. And then there was a terrible loud noise, and I seen that he was flat dead on the floor. He warn't moving no more.

Me and Miguel looked at each other then, but we didn't say nuthin for a minute. Then he looked back at the door to the room where Ms. Douglas and Miss Watson sleep.

"Stay right there," he says to me.

"But—"

He didn't answer me but jus' went to their door and pushed it open a little bit and went in there.

"No, no." It was just a whisper. I heard some noises in there, and then Miguel come back out. He had blood on him now.

"Are they okay?" I asked him, quiet-like. But he didn't answer. There was a phone in the hallway there, and Miguel picked it up.

"*¡¿Que paso?! ¡¿Como sucedió todo ésto?!*" He was talking to hisself. And I was talking to myself too in a way. My brain was blinkering through everything that had come. I thought about them nice ladies that hadn't done no harm and had only tried to help me. I thought about Pap who was my own blood flying through the air and then crashing down on the floor down below. And I thought about Miguel who had saved my life. I seen it all in my brain, but it was fuzzy like, most like it warn't real.

Miguel he was still on the phone, a-waiting for an answer. And then finally there was somebody there. "We need an ambulance," he says.

CHAPTER 14

The Rattlesnake-skin Does Its Work

MIGUEL didn't say nuthin after he got off the phone, but he went straight downstairs and out the door and into the rain. I followed him fast behind and didn't even check if Pap was still dead, but you'll prob'ly say I shoulda made good and sure after you hear the full story. Miguel was in a hurry though, and I didn't catch up to him until he was out the front door and going 'round the back of the house. He was hurrying most like he didn't care about me no more.

"Miguel," I yelled. But he didn't say nuthin back until I catched him and grabbed him from behind. It was hard to talk and hear in all that rain.

"Where are you going?"

"I can't be here when the police come." He turned to go again, but I didn't understand what he was saying.

"But why? You didn't do nuthin," I tell him. "Are you a drug dealer?" That's all the reason I could think of at a time like that.

He stopped. "No, *muchacho*. I'm not a drug dealer." And he said it most like I had hurt him. "*Soy illegal*. My parents brought me here when I was just a boy."

"But you saved me," I said.

"It is no matter to them. They will send me away. My daughter needs a father. I have to go now."

And now I seen it clear. Pap had mixed everything up, just like he always done before. He took everything good and turned it to bad, and it gave me a sick feeling in my stomach to know that I was kin to a man like that. And that warn't all. I was also blameful for touching that snakeskin and carrying it back to Miguel before I knowed any better. I catched up to Miguel in his little room, and I watched him grab just a few of his things but left behind most of it. Last thing he took was the photogram of his wife and his little girl. And it made a body feel awful low-down to see him do it.

Then he went to the stable and started getting Carolina ready to ride. I reckoned that he was gonna use her for his escape, on account she was the best and fastest horse we had in the stable. But when he brung her out into the rain, we saw the 'copter overhead, coming up fast. It had its spotlamp on and looked like it was headed in our direction. Carolina warn't no match for a 'copter, and Miguel he knowed it too.

"You won't make it over the hill," I told him. And from his look he knowed I was right. He must've been thinking of his daughter then, 'cause he looked awful stuck, like there warn't no way out for him. And then I struck a notion in my brain.

"I got another idea," I says to him, and even now the 'copter was near right a'top of us, though they hadn't found us with their light yet. "Follow me!"

Well he warn't too keen on it and delayed a bit, but then he made to tie Carolina up so as she wouldn't run off, and we both gave her a pat on the back, which was all we could muster for a goodbye right then. You'da thunk that we'd be sad at a time like that, sad for Carolina, but also for Ms. Douglas and Miss Watson. And somewheres inside we was real sad. But being sad on the outside ain't always possible, and we was in a difficult predictament wherein Miguel's whole life was in danger of being taken away by the 'thorities, so we'd have to wait to show ourselves on the outside how sad we was on the inside.

Afore you knowed it, I was on the trail and I could hear Miguel following behind. I went straight for the wooded part, where the 'copter wouldn't be able to follow us so good on account of all the trees.

"The creek! We have to make it to the creek!" I looked back to make sure he was still following fast behind. "It'll take us all the way down to the river. It's the fastest way out. It'll take us all the way to the ocean."

We followed the creek downhill and come out where it ran into that big pipe that was half in the ground and half out, the one I told you about before. "See here!" I had to shout to make him hear me over the rain and the sirens, 'cause there was sirens now too, and they was getting closer. Miguel went right past me and I seen that I had persuaded him good that this was the best way to get away. But he turned back to me.

"Thank you, Huck. *Eren un amigo de adeveras.* A true friend for me." And now I got what he was driving at. He was saying goodbye to me without really saying it straight.

"I'm coming with you," I says and real firm too, so as to cut off any argumentation.

"No, it's too dangerous, *muchacho.* I might not see my family for—"

Then I struck on it. "My friend Tom, his aunt is a lawyer," I tell him. "She can help you!" I warn't sure it was true right then, but I was in the business of giving Miguel something to hope about and also make him think again 'bout his decision to leave me behind with the 'thorities.

The 'copter was getting closer again now and it was even harder to hear. The blue and red lights was flashing through the trees and even blinkered on Miguel's face for a time. I watched him close, and his face was full of seriosity. I could tell the situation was pulling him in at least two different directions. But then he got hard and cold with me.

"No one can help me now," he says. "Except me. Go home, Huck! I don't want you here." He was lying, you see, but he thought he was doing right by me. That's the easiest time to lie, when you think you're doing good by someone and not bad. Right away I seen it warn't no use in arguing to change his brain. He was a-gonna go and leave me behind and who knows where I'd go or who

I'd end up with. So I did what you or anybody would do in that type of situation. I squirmed right past him, like I done with Pap a thousand time before, and straight down into that pipe. I crawled in quick before he could say anything.

"I ain't got no home," I told him when I got my head turned 'round. He looked right torn then, like I was putting him in an awful spot, and I felt bad a little for what I'd done, but mostly not. As I 'spected, it worked good enough, because he 'ventually got down and followed me into that pipe.

He had to crawl in there 'cause it was so short for a full-size man, and it warn't burbly like before but more noisy, as the water was rushing all around us. At another

time, it might have scared me good, but these was special circumstantials. I reckoned I was free of Pap now, so we only jus' had to stay clear of the 'thorities. But I reckoned wrong, as you'll soon know when I tell the rest. With a man like Pap, you can't never be sure he's dead enough.

Well, as you may have heard about, there was a lamp at the end of that tunnel. But it warn't a bright lamp or a big lamp but just a half a circle of gray blue that got a little bit bigger the longer we went along in there. It was dismal dark, and Miguel didn't say nuthin on account he was thinking about the ladies back at the house or maybe his daughter who he might never see no more. But I could hear him breathalyzing behind me. We was going as fast as we could.

'Ventually we come falling out of that pipe and into the river as they call it. It was just like Tom Sawyer had showed me, a big concrete ditch but the sides was straight up here instead of slanty. There was lots of water now but not enough that we couldn't walk along the edge with the water rushing about our feet and even up over our waists. We stayed real close to the side so that it'd be hard for anybody to see us without which he was specially looking for a couple of fugitives.

Miguel made another effort at telling me that I couldn't come along.

"You have to go back," he says. But it warn't his choice to make.

"I ain't gonna leave you here all alone. I'm going to take you to Tom Sawyer and his Aunt Polly. She'll know what to do."

"There's nothing left to do but run."

"Then I'll run with you." And I just started walking down river, in the direction the water was going. "C'mon."

'Ventually he realized there warn't no way for him to stop me from coming. He was a smart Mexigrant and he knowed that—if he tried anything to get free of me—I just woulda run up ahead or follow him from behind. And he couldn't ask for nobody to help him on account he was illegal and now on the run from the law. I knowed I was taking 'vantage of the situation, and you might think that it woulda made me feel bad about it, but I was thinking about Miguel mostly. I reckoned that he needed the company and that maybe I'd be able to make myself useable to him. On my account this was just the 'venture that I was looking for, though I did feel a bit of meloncholera on account of Miguel's situation and what happened to Ms. Douglas and Miss Watson. I hoped to myself that they was okay and that the 'thorities would take real good care of them instead of just chasing us who ain't done nuthin wrong except handling a snakeskin.

We walked a considerable long ways that night. First we went down the concrete part of river and under a bridge, which was most like a tunnel. After a time, we come out to a place where it was more like a proper creek again with overgrown weeds and mud. Then there was a ramp that took us back down to the concrete, and the river was shaped like a V here with the slanted walls, and we walked right down the middle with water rushing past us that was most up to my waist. We heard a coyote howling in the dark and the rain, and it was a lonesome sound.

After a time, we come to a part where the sides of the river was straight up like walls, and it most felt like we was underground 'cept you could still see the sky but not much more. The water was lower here on account that the channel was wider. There was fantastical drawings on the walls, but they was old and some of the paint had gotten washed away so as you couldn't tell exactly what they was pictures of. Pretty soon our section joined up with another section, and water come rushing in so that it was deeper now, but we was still able to walk. Miguel said that we was in what they called the proper river now, and no more in the creek. You wouldn't think it was possible, but we passed a big clump of pussy willows that was growing up out of the concrete like they couldn't even tell that

this warn't a proper muddy riverbank. Miguel said it was
a sign that living things had a way of surviving no matter
what their circumstantials was. He said there was prob'ly a
little crack somewhere in the concrete where they'd found
their way down to proper soil.

We was all alone, and nobody seemed to be looking
in the river. Still, it didn't feel real comfortable to be down
there, on account there was nowheres to go if somebody
was to see us. We was most like squatting ducks. Neither
one of us said anything 'bout it, but I felt it, and I could
tell that Miguel did too. The other thing was that our vi-
suality warn't very good down there. There warn't no way
to see if the policecops was closing in or whether we was
free and clear.

A couple of times we passed conjunctions where another river met up with this one and dumped in a whole
bunch more water. Every time we did it, the water got
deeper and faster. It started out underneath my knees but
then passed 'em pretty quick. And afore I knowed it, the
water was up 'round my waist again, and it was harder to
walk. Miguel was real knowledgeful of the local geogerphy, so he knowed the names of all the creeks and could
keep track of how far we'd come. Calabasas, Browns Canyon, Aliso Canyon, Caballero. They was just names to me,
and some was even Mexigrant names, but it was comfortable to know that we warn't lost.

We come to a place where there was a bunch of iron
rings you could use as a ladder to get out, so I clumb up
real quick and took a peek. All I seen was houses along
the river, and policecop lights flashing a way far off in the

distance. We turned it over a bit and talked about maybe leaving the river, but Miguel said he reckoned our chances was better down there. If we was to come out, we was likely to be seen by somebody walking down the street or crossing through their backyard, and they might tell the policecops. So we kept a-walking down in the river, even as it got deeper even up to my chest. But Miguel had holt of my hand tight, so there warn't no danger that I would float away.

Me and Miguel took for cover under a bridge that night. It was tough at first, 'cause we walked under a couple of bridges where there was trolls living there and warn't no room for a couple of fugitives. We got spooked real good by one particular troll that was living up under a bridge but was hidden real good so as me and Miguel didn't see her till we was right up close and her face come out of the dark like a bear coming out of a cave where she'd been hibernapping. She meant to scare us and she did too. Her face was all gnarled up like a gorgon, and her hair was wild like it was made of snakes. She made a sound like a bear, and Miguel and me went away without even saying we was sorry, on account we didn't know if trolls could understand people talk.

But 'ventually we found one bridge where there warn't no trolls to bother us. There was an awful snug part right up where the bridge hit the shore, and we was able to hide ourselves pretty good. Up above we heard a bunch of sirens and even some voices once, but nobody thought to look under that bridge. There was all sorts of stuff there, stuff that other folk would call trash, but that made it seem like a special place to me. The regular kind of trash was there, like beer cans, but less normal stuff too, like a shopping car turned upside down, and a truck tire half buried 'neath the ground. We was a-quivering up there on account it was so cold and wet, but we couldn't hardly notice after all the things that had come to pass that night.

Pretty soon me and Miguel both fell asleep. I was so tired I only waked up one time but right away I wished I hadn't. There was a lady down by the water, and she was all in white. She seemed to be looking for something or somebody. I thought maybe she was a-crying. It was awful ghostful. I closed my eyes and when I opened 'em up again she was already gone. Well, it spooked me good and showed me right away what kind of river this was.

Pap Comes Back
from the Dead

I waked up real early, before the rest of Los Angeles. And there was a funny-looking bird staring in at us. It was monstrous tall and kinda blue gray with a black and white head and a long yellow beak. He looked like the type of bird you would see if you went to Mars on a spaceship and went down to one of the strange red rivers they have there. When I opened my eyes, he was right there looking at me, like to ask what we was doing there and where we was going. But he didn't stay to hear my answer. He only just let out a horrible squawk and flew off down the river. Well that was enough to wake up Miguel.

Miguel wanted to get moving down river right away. He said that it was better to walk before the sun was all the way up and people was out and about and likely to see us down there and tell the 'thorities. We had to find a better place to hide. So we walked like we had the night before, huddled close to the side and wading through the rushing water. It had stopped raining but the clouds was still up there, a-threatening to drop more any time they had the inclination.

A couple hour run along and there started to be more cars and even some bicycles. Just in time we come to a place where it changed from all concrete to a kind of woods. It warn't a proper woods though but even more eery and ghostful. There was all sorts of papers and cloth hanging from the trees, and there was a couple of stumpy little palm trees not at all like the ones that are as tall as a mountain. And there was all sorts of trash all over the ground, and I thought maybe this is where the garbage trucks come to drop all the trash from all the people in California. But Miguel said no, it was just the trash that was in the street that got washed down there in the rain and then stuck in the trees or a-scattered all over the ground. In just a couple minutes, I seen three more shopping cars turned upside down, and the 'luminum cap of a trash can that would make for a bully shield in a saber fight, and 'bout twenty shoes but always only one and never in a pair, and even a brand-new computer, half in the water and half out. If a body didn't know better, he woulda thought that there had been a funicular war, and me and Miguel was the last two people on earth, scrounging around for food and a place to sleep amidst all the trash.

If you was the type of person that would want to search through a trash bin for hidden treasure, well this was the river for you. Miguel reckoned that it warn't all like this, but this was just the spot where all the trash got catched up, being the first part with trees and branches that would act like a kind of net—so the parts further down would be less trash-like. This is my chance I thought, so I picked up the most strangest thing I could find as a keepsafe—it was a little bald eagle that looked most like it had been attached to a statuary of some type, but he didn't have any feet, and his wing was breaked halfway off, and the paint on his body was chipped everywhere pretty good. You woulda felt sorry for him, but he still had a 'spression that was monstrous proud, so it didn't seem so bad to me. I showed him to Miguel and told him that now we had a pet eagle to take on our 'venture with us and maybe he'd give us good luck to weigh against the bad luck brung by the snakeskin. Miguel he was suspeptical, I could tell. But he tried to act bully about it on my account.

Once we was a little ways in, Miguel found a spot in the trees that was covered real good and we set down to wait for it to come dark. We both lay out on the muddy ground even though it was cold and wet. I seen Miguel use somebody's old sweater for a pillow, so I found a couple of articulars of clothing and did the same. It remembered me of when I was hiding out in the woods back home, living in my little lean-to and trying to get free of Pap, only this time I warn't alone.

I asked Miguel to tell me the story of how he come to America, but he warn't in the proper mood to tell a story just then. So we was both quiet and still. We fell asleep and slept off most of the day, making up for the sleep we didn't get the night before. That's how it is when things change awful sudden and hard. You need to sleep more than you would at a more regular time, and it takes you a far sight longer to wake up. But when you do wake up, you might feel a little more comfortable about where you are and all the changes that come.

Miguel was still asleep when I waked up, so I went exploring through the bushes and trash. It was already coming dark. There on the river we was setting below the rest of the city. A big bridge that was just for buses crossed near right over us, and every now and again a big city bus would go roaring overhead, but they didn't pay no tension to what was below. There was a large flat area at the bottom of the river, but there was big concrete ramps on either side, and I could see the lights of a baseball field up on the right. Every once in a while I'd hear a monstrous loud clank and I'd know that somebody just got a hit, and a good 'un if there was cheers right after. I clumb up the side of the river and got to the fence where I could look through to see 'em playing baseball. They was older yet than me, and some of 'em was awful good. The grass was still wet and soggy, but it played alright. And there was all sort of people watching the game from the bleachers, prob'ly the mamas and paps of the fellows who was playing, and other such people that wanted one team to win, or t'other. I wondered then whether my life might ever be like that, jus' normal like with baseball games and ice cream cones and such. I supposed prob'ly not, but I warn't ready to give up all hope of it. In a way, I figgered that's what I had with them two ladies and Miguel and even Carolina, but didn't notice as I was too busy getting used to it. But there warn't no way to get back to that now, so I tried not to think on it.

Pretty soon I seen a policecop walking around. He hadn't seen me yet, but I figgered that I'd better remove any chance that he might. So I clumb back over the fence and down to the river. On my way back to get Miguel, I found a big mound of junk, most like somebody was using it for a dumping ground. After hunting around for a bit, I found something that struck an idea in my brain.

I waked up Miguel and brung him back to the junk-yard, and I showed him what I found—a couple of in-nertubes like from the inside of a truck tire. I had it in my brain that we would each get in one of them and float down the river together, most like we was on a prop-er holiday like rich folk. But Miguel was digging around at something else—an old wooden garage door that was sticking out from the bottom.

Well I bet you guessed it already but we fashioneered a bully raft out of that door and those tubes. On account of his work with the horses, Miguel knowed how to make stuff strong and tight, so as it would work for a watercraft. Before you knowed it we was floating down the river in a powerful style. There was room enough for the both of us and then some. Under different circumstantials, you might have even thought that it was a 'joyable way to spend an evening.

And Miguel was right, the garbage cleaned up pretty good soon enough, and before you knowed it the river turns real pretty, most like a proper river back home, but more narrower. There was parts you would even forget that you was in a monstrous big city like Los Angeles. All along the river there was trolls living in the shadows, but these was tent trolls and not bridge trolls. Most of 'em was still sleeping, but some had fires going and we could hear their troll talk, but not real clear. We passed under a car bridge and it got all dark and green and glowy on account of some slimy stuff that was growing on the water. And the smell was an awful strange smell. Well it warn't the first or the last thing that gave me the fantods on our trip, but it was awful ghostful.

I started to say something to Miguel, but he didn't even notice. I seen him then looking at that picture of his family. Miguel was thinking about his wife and little girl, up yonder in Arizona, and he was low and homesick, you could tell. I do believe he cared just as much for his people just like someone born here legal and proper. Some people might not believe it, but I reckon it's so. It got me feeling all mean and lowdown, on account that my Pap was the one who done it all. And I got even more decided that I would help Miguel any ways that I could, even if I was only Huck.

So I got out at the front of the raft now, like a real navigator. I'd even pulled a long pole up out of the muck

to use as a steering rudder. I steered us 'round a family of strange ducks there, black and white, not like the ducks back home. And they made a noise to let us know that we warn't to bother them again if we could help it. There was turkles too, most like the mud turkles we had in the river back home. They was laying out on the rocks but would dive into the water afore we got to them, so we didn't get to see 'em up close. And one time I even saw a fish in the water. It was at least two foot long and didn't seem scared of our little raft at all. Then there was a big white bird that was on the river. We spooked him good, and he lifted up into the air real gracious like and swopped off into the trees. Miguel said he was a special waterbird called an egret that was one of the most beautiful kind.

We come up fast on some rapids, and it was bully by me. You see, the big river back home don't really have proper rapids on account it's so big. Rapids is more natural to happen in a place where a river is small, and all the water's got to push through a narrow spot. Well that's what this was, and there was rocks there too. Our homemade raft did pretty good and didn't neither get stuck, and it gave us a push in a way so as now we was moving faster down the river. A little ways further there was some more rapids, only these ones we couldn't float over on account it was too shallow. So me and Miguel took the raft up out of the water and carried her to the other side where it was smooth again.

There was places on the shore where the plants was so dense you couldn'ta gone on the land even if you wanted to. And then there was other places where it would open up a little bit and there'd be the tiniest bit of river beach with just a spot of sand where there might be a mud turkle resting. We pulled over at one spot, and I clumb up the riverbank and through the brush so as to do a scouting expedition. But it was only a golf course up there, which don't serve well for fugitives on account there's nowheres to hide. But I did find one bully orange golf ball that I kept in my pocket as a keepsafe. On my way back down to the raft, I got all scraped up by the bushes but didn't mind. I had to be careful of the spiders that was everywhere. I most ran straight into one that was so big and yellow he must've been the poisonous kind and woulda killed me dead if I'd a given him the smallest chance. But instead I went 'round through some other bushes and left him on his own.

'Ventually we floated on by a group of folks who was living down by the river. The sun had already gone full down, and they was in the water washing theyselves and their clothes. One of them fellows looked up and was awful happy to see us floating by. He didn't lack for a shortage of teeth.

"It's Captain Ahab!" he says. And his friend, who was a black woman with her hair all done up in braids, she says, "And Quequeeg too!" I don't know it for sure but I think they was comparing us to a couple of famous pirates. All the rest of them people looked up when we passed. So I waved at 'em and smiled—that's the best way to make friendly like—and they all waved back at us. Well I turned back as they went by, and I watched 'em all as they got smaller and smaller, and I thought that maybe prob'ly I'd never see them again or come to know why they was living down in the river, 'stead of up top with the regular folk. It remembered me of my situation back home when I went to live in the lean-to. Maybe they had their own troubles with their own Paps.

After a while I was feeling all bully about our progress and about how we'd evaded the 'thorities. So I reckoned I'd try to help Miguel feel a bit better, and I says, "I reckon we're making pretty good time." Well he looked up at me and jus' in time too, 'cause his eyes got big and scared.

"Huck!" he yells, and I didn't know what he was driving at. "Get down!"

Well then I heard a loud crack, and I knowed right away that we was being shot at. My first idea was that it was the 'thorities, but I looked behind me, where Miguel was looking, and I seen the camper right away. It was parked on a car bridge overlooming the river, and my Pap was standing there with his shotgun. It didn't seem possible, but there he was. And he was a-trying to kill us both dead. I figgered right away what had happened. Pap warn't dead like we thought and must've survived the fall, just like he survived all the other stuff that had tried to kill him. And somehow he must've heard me and Miguel head for the river. It didn't seem possible, but that's how it was with Pap. I couldn't never get rid of him.

There was another crack, and the bullet hit the corner of our raft, and the back tube let out a big sigh and a hiss. Me and Miguel didn't even have to say nuthin atwixt us—we both jumped into the water so Pap wouldn't have so much of a target to aim for. I come up and grabbed one corner of the raft, but Miguel warn't nowheres to be seen no more. I was looking for him all over, but he warn't nowheres I could see.

All the while I'm drifting closer and closer to the bridge without no way to stop, which is not the direction I want to be going. Pap is trying to aim, but the closer I get to right up under him, the harder he's got to angle it. So I got one thing working for me and one thing working against me. He fired one more time, but this time he missed altogether on account of the angle.

And then I hear Miguel. "The trees, Huck! Over there!" He was come up on t'other side of the raft and he was kicking and thrashing like a catfish stuck on a hook.

He was trying to pull us over to the side where there was more cover, so I started kicking too and we managed to get out of Pap's viewpoint and under the trees. And we floated under the bridge, where it was quiet. But we knowed that he was gonna run over to the other side and try to get us again. He's not one to give up on a couple murders after just one chance. Well we got a break, the trees was thick there, and he couldn't see us well enough to get another shot. He knowed we was down there though, 'cause we could hear him a-yelling. "I'll kill you both when I git a hold of you! A no-good, stealin' son and a damned illegal Mexigrant. I'll kill you both, I swear I will."

The raft was all a-kilter on account of the tube losing all its air, so Miguel and I just swam along beside it. We didn't say nuthin but we made a connection with our eyes, and we both knowed what we was thinking. First of all, Pap was a tough one and hadn't died from that fall. Second thing, he must've been a-following us when we went into the woods. I guess it made some sense. If he warn't full dead, he warn't neither gonna hang around for the 'thorities to arrive. He must've heard us make for the river. It was hard to believe, but I told you how smart he was, 'specially when he got worked up good about something that seemed like it warn't fair to him.

After a time we come out to an open area and we reckoned that we had enough of a lead on Pap that we could stop to fix our raft. There was a sandy bank there, like a beach, and an old man was sitting in a lawn chair with a fishing pole. In fact, he was reeling in a little fish jus' as we dragged the raft up on to the sand. He warn't flabbergassed at all to see us come out of the woods but just watched us—most like it was normal for a couple of fugitives to come floating by after the sun was going down. So I took a chance.

"Hey mister," I says. "You got anywheres we can hide?"

He didn't answer for a minute but took his time taking the hook out of the fish's mouth. He dumped the fish in a bucket, and I seen then that there was 'bout three or four fish in there, not big ones but not tiny neither. This latest one was immediously thrashing about on account he didn't know that he was stuck yet and there warn't no easy way out of that bucket, whereas his brothers was more calm having grown accustomated to their predictament and biding their time till they could get a better chance to 'scape.

The old man looked us over and finally decided on how to answer. "They call me the Colonel. Four years in the Fertile Crescent and all my country gave me was this lousy nickname."

It warn't an answer straight on, but I took it in a friendly way. "We're awful thirsty, too."

"In the midst of the biggest gulley washer in forty years, and the boy says he needs water."

I understood now that he was the type of man who liked to talk and meant to stretch out the conversation with commentaries and reflections. That was bully by me, as long as we might negotiate something in return for the trouble of listening.

"You got any water?"

"C'mon back into my humble abode. I got plenty of water back here." He pointed back behind him where there was a gap in the trees, and there was a blue tarp strung up for a kind of roof. "In fact, what d'ya say you stick around and join me for a late dinner. It looks like you might need the meal, and I won't turn down the company."

We was awful hungry, so neither one of us was inclined to say no. It was like a proper home back in there with a little area set up for the Colonel to sleep and an old beat-up chair, most like the one I found in the desert. I reckoned the Colonel lived down there, and it got me sentimentering about my little lean-to back in Missouri. I reckon just 'bout anywheres can work for a home, if a body ain't too particular.

Within just a couple minutes, the Colonel had a couple of those fish a-hissin' and a-poppin' on the fire, and me and Miguel was eyeing 'em like they was the last fish on the earth after the pock-a-lips. It didn't take long till they was all brown and crispified, and the Colonel gave us first chance. "Have at 'em, boys!" he says. And we did.

"Thanks, Mr. Colonel," I says, but it was all garbled up on account I was trying to eat the fish. Miguel was pretty quiet, prob'ly 'cause he was afeard of getting recognified by the Colonel. The Colonel didn't care though. He jus' kept talking.

"You think they'll get the Dodger game in? Seems like rain in Los Angeles is like my mama and her old man. On again, off again. On again, off again." He didn't mean for us to answer him, so we didn't.

The Colonel had a little radio going, and at first it was playing pretty piano music, like from the old times. And it was a good songtrack for the Colonel's talk. But pretty soon a man come on to tell the news, and that's where me and Miguel realized that we was famous, but not in the way that a body would want to be.

It started with talk about baseball that had nuthin to do with us. You see, it was the opening days of the season, and there was all such optimystical talk as you hear before the season starts, and only later is when people start complaining about how lousy and lowdown all the players is. I knowed that Miguel was a big fanatic about the Dodgers—that's what them people in Los Angeles call their baseball players—and I could see that it lightened him up a bit to hear baseball talk. But they was saying that the game might could be delayed on account of all the rain. I always thought the best time to play a sport was in the middle of a rainpour, 'cause it gets all muddy and slippery and nobody can't control where the ball goes. But I guess some folk feel differently.

Then come another fellow on the radio, talking about the cars and the roads. "And that sigalert out on the 405, just south of the 10, has turned into a real clusterdoodle. If you're headed north, you might want to consider a hot air balloon or a jetski." I know it's strange, but that's how the radio folk talk in California.

And then another fellow come on to talk. "Thanks, Mike. We'll come back to you in ten minutes for another update." And then here it come. "I want to update you on a troubling story we've been following all morning long. Authorities are still looking for an illegal Mexican immigrant who kidnapped a young boy in Bell Canyon last night."

Me and Miguel looked at each other then. We tried to

hide it, but I think the Colonel seen it. And I started worrying that he was formulating all the wrong conclusions.

"He's also wanted in the brutal stabbing of two women, one of whom is in critical condition at Valley Hospital." Miguel he made a cross then. He was sad then—I could see it right clear.

"Congressman Buck Harkness spoke at a press conference a half hour ago, condemning the nation's lax immigration policies—"

Now there was another voice on the radio. He was saying stuff like Pap would say, but not in a lowdown ornery way that Pap would, but like someone who'd had a proper education and was learned how to talk like a lawyer or a perfesser.

"This horrific crime is a reminder of just how dangerous these people are. They are law breakers. And violent criminals. If we can't keep them out of our country, then no matter how safe we feel, we will never be truly safe—"

Before he could get done with his speech, the Colonel got up and turned it off.

"How's the fish, boys?" he says to me and Miguel, most like he hadn't heard nuthin.

"Miguel he didn't do it, Mr. Colonel sir. He saved me. And he tried to help Ms. Douglas and Miss Watson." That's what I told him.

"I didn't say he did anything," says the Colonel back. "They've been talking about you boys all day long here on the squawkbox."

"So you knowed it was us all along?"

"I had my suspicions."

"It was my Pap, Colonel sir. He was the one who done it. He gets awful drunk and mean." The Colonel nodded most like he understood what I meant. "They're coming after us, ain't they?"

"I imagine they are. If this fellow Harkness had his way, there'd likely be a lynching. But I don't want any part of that business, boys. I've seen enough killing in my life. You boys are welcome to lay low here for a bit and then be on your way. Whenever you've had your fill of these delicious Los Angeles carp."

Miguel finally started to get comfortable and to think that maybe the Colonel wouldn't turn us in. "Our raft— she is broken."

"I saw that. I've got some tar here that I use to re-pair holes in my roof. That should work to get her seaworthy again."

Well Miguel got to work straight away. And the Col-onel talked while Miguel was heating up the tar. He told all about the river, which he knowed all about, it being his home. It warn't always concrete but had once been wild and meambling, just like a river back home.

"It was 1938, boys. That's when the big flood came. Of course, that was before my time, but I've seen the pictures. This river, the one you're escaping down, spilled out and killed over a hundred people."

"Will it flood again, Colonel sir?" I asked him. "There's been an awful sight of rain the last couple days."

"Never again, son. The army came in and did what the army always does. They solved one problem and created about a dozen new ones in its place. They put in all this concrete that you see and made sure that the river stayed put, not like the old days when it would spill out all over the city. They tried to tame the river, and they did a pretty good job of it. But the wild things in this world have a way of coming back. And that's what's happened in all these many years."

I told him that we'd seen some of them wild things already, but he said there was even more to see if we kept our eyes and brains open to it. He said that a long time ago there was bears—the golden kind—and deer and beavers and even wolves. But there was still bobcats and coyotes and other wild critters. There used to be trout as big as a grown man's arm, but now they was all gone, so what we was eating was carp, which was the most common type in the river nowadays, and pretty good for eating too.

Miguel was finishing up the tar job, and he used a burning log to seal it up good. He warn't barely listening on account he was working on fixing the problem with our raft. That's always how it was at the stables too. Miguel was always a-working, 'cause that's what made him Miguel and not some other fellow.

I asked the Colonel what would happen to us if we was catched by the 'thorities. He said he didn't know right off, and he got real quiet while he thought about it some. Then he started up again.

"I reckon that most men are cowards, boys. They're scared of what they don't understand. And this fellow Harkness, he's the type of man who preys on the fear of the mob. He gets 'em all riled up with talk of trouble and danger. The average man doesn't like trouble and danger.

He doesn't want to take the time to get the facts straight and figure out what justice is. He just wants someone to tell him that the trouble and danger are gone, that there's nothing to worry about anymore.

"I was born and raised in the East, and I've lived in the West now for a good many years, so I know the average all around. The average man's a coward. He doesn't like trouble and danger. But if only half a man—like this Buck Harkness fellow—shouts 'Lynch him! Lynch him!' the average man's not going to raise his voice up and object. No, he's going to go along and ride the coattails of this half-a-man.

"Let me tell you something else, boys. There isn't any way to avoid trouble and danger in this life. You've got to accept that first. When it comes, you face up to it, best you can. But there isn't any use in trying to avoid it. It's a-coming, just as sure as the rain."

Miguel said thank you and that remembered me to do the same.

"Thank you for the fish, Mr. Colonel, sir," I says to him.

"I'm no sir. I'm just a man," he says back. "They call me Colonel. But I'm just a man, just like your friend Miguel, just like you're on your way to being."

We was drifting now, and he was still going.

"You boys take care of yourselves now. If they're gonna get you, they're gonna get you. Don't worry yourselves about it too much. Just stick together. Trouble and danger aren't meant for a man to face alone."

Well it was past the middle of the night now. Miguel

had worked straight through, and there was just beginning to be the glow of the sun out in the east. We woulda been tired if we hadn'ta slept all day long. Me and Miguel figgered we could float down a ways before the sun come up to where you could see it. I looked back at the Colonel and I seen him set back down in his chair as we was on our way. I guess he warn't ready to sleep yet. He seemed a little sad to see us float away. I hoped that it wouldn't be too long before a couple of different fugitives would float down and keep him company and maybe listen to his bully speeches for a time.

CHAPTER 16

What More Trouble Come from Handling the Snakeskin

WE was quiet again for a while, and I reckon that atwixt the two of us we was both thinking about what the Colonel said and cogitating on what might be coming up ahead for us. It woulda been bully and comfortable to think that mayhaps we might have seen the last of Pap, but there warn't but a small chance of that. He meant to kill us, and the rabies had holt of him good. It warn't likely that he'd just find some other way to disseminate his days, at least not until he was able to finish the job he started or get hisself killed in the trying.

I turned it over in my brain for a little bit, and I bet Miguel was doing the same. We could leave the river, but there was lots of people looking for us and we'd be more likely to run into the 'thorities. Or we could stay down on the river and take our chances that we might bump into old Pap again. It warn't a good choice at all. But that's how it is sometime. You don't always got no choice about what choices you got to make. And if you don't make a choice, that's just the same as making one

anyway. So there's no easy way to get out of it, 'cept by doing the best you can.

Well we floated so good and slow and quiet you'd most think that we was on a pleasure cruise and not fugitives from the law. The sun was real slow in coming up, and I must've fallen asleep for a time it was so peaceable. But I waked up when I heard Miguel.

"Look, *muchacho*," says he. He was pointing up at the sky, where there was a bird soaring over us most like to look over us and protect us. It had stopped raining altogether. "It's a hawk," Miguel says. *"Gavilán colirrojo."* It was beautiful the way he said it, and I tried to say it back but it come out all rough and bejarbled. Pap said that Mexigrants warn't smart enough to learn how to speak proper English, but I reckon it ain't true, 'cause I heard how good and beautiful Miguel could talk when he had something he wanted to say.

I watched the *gavilán*—it was really a hawk but I decided that I could call it by its name that Miguel used. It remembered me of the little eagle I'd found and still had in my pocket for to bring us good luck, and I thought maybe the two birds was connected in some way. The *gavilán* was riding along on the wind monstrous proud and comfortable, and I wondered what she could see from

up there, besides the two of us fugitives on our little raft.
Prob'ly all the city lights like we saw from the hill on our
first morning in Los Angeles. There was too many dark
clouds though, so she prob'ly couldn't see the ocean that
day. She swooped back over us and took a perch in an oak
tree where she could look down on us and everybody else
in the city. I had to turn back to keep an eye on her, and
that's when I seen something else in the sky.

A 'copter.

Miguel saw it too. It was just a light in the sky, but
we knowed what it was right away. It was too low to be
a proper aeroplane. It stayed small for a time, but pretty
soon it was getting bigger as it come nearer to us. In fact, it
was aimed most directly at us, and we knowed that they'd
found us now and there warn't nowheres to run. Pretty
soon we could hear the hum of the blades, and then that
hum become a proper thwuppin' noise of a 'copter, most
like it was coming to hunt us down.

It was most right over us now.

Well we was both scared but I struck an idea. I tossed
Miguel some of the Colonel's blankets.

"Get underneath!" I told him. "Quick!" I seen him
tuck hisself under the cloth, and I took one and hid under
it too. I peaked out from underneath as it got near, and I
could see that it was a policecop 'copter, which made my
heart jump back up into my lungs. And the thwuppin' was
near on earsplicing on account they was right over us now,
and I couldn't help but think on Miguel's little girl and
how it warn't right that her father would be captivated by
the policecops and sent back to Mexico. I didn't think that

the blankets would do much good to hide us, but it was near on the only thing we could do.

But then, just when the sound was the loudest, it seemed that maybe the thwuppin' faded just a little. I stuck my head out again, and I seen that the 'copter had flown right over the top of us and hadn't even stopped. It was already way out yonder on the way to somewheres else. They hadn't seen us at all. Well my heart just about burst with happiness then. We both of us set up and hove off our camouflage blankets.

"They didn't see us!" I yelled.

"*Muchacho*—" he says in a whisper. Miguel was smiling too, but just for a second. I seen his face change from a smile to something else.

"We're home free, Miguel! By tomorrow or the next day we'll be down to the ocean."

"Be very still. Do not move." His voice was quiet and full of seriosity. That's when I heard the rattle. I turned and saw it. There was a rattlesnake on the Colonel's blanket he'd given us. The snake must've been sleeping in there, and he warn't none too happy to be disturbed. He was so close to me I could've reached down to touch him if he was more friendly like. But he was ready to strike me dead, and now my heart really jumped.

Time went frozen then. I stayed still like a statue, and Miguel didn't move neither. It might've been just a second or two but it seemed like whole days and nights come and gone. I didn't want to move, but I warn't right comfortable, and after a time I just couldn't help it. It was my instinctuals taking over, but it warn't the right time. My foot

moved just a little bit, and the snake he lunged out for me.

But Miguel was too quick. He threw one of the other old blankets out, just at the right time, and the snake's head disappeared into the cloth instead of biting my leg. Miguel gathered it all up most quick like he was an A-rab snake handler or some such. He didn't say nuthin but stepped over to the side and threw the blanket—with the snake inside—overboard, just like a pirate would've done with one of his enemies. Only Miguel made a little sound—like a yelp—when he let go.

The snake and the blanket went splash in the water. And I looked up at Miguel who had saved my life all over again.

"I think he got me," says Miguel. He was a-holding his hand, and there was a little red mark on his wrist, where the snake had bit him.

CHAPTER 17

Making a Deal with a Rapscallion

WE got off the river then, pulled up under a bridge like before, and I hid the raft 'round the other side of a pillar. There was a dark place up under there, and it looked like some people had lived there at one time, but it had been empty for a good while, at least that's what we thought. Miguel laid down—he couldn't stand no more. And his hand was turning blue and even black.

"I'm a-going for help," I says.

"No, they will send me away. I will never see my family again."

"But you need a doctor."

"There is a medicine. *Antivenin.* We kept it at the stable."

"But it's too far. I can't go back there."

"The hospital. Find a hospital. They will have it." I started to go, but he pulled me back. "Hurry, *muchacho*. I need to take it in the next couple of hours, or it will get very bad for me. You understand?" I didn't answer him but just nodded. I could tell he was afeard.

"Thank you, Huck. You are my friend, my *hermano*."

He closed his eyes, but I couldn't tell if he was knocked out or just sleeping. So I left him there. There was a splinter of light coming down, so I aimed for that and clumb up the concrete to get out of the river. I come up in the middle of a big road where the cars was zipping by on either side like there warn't even no river right down below. I had to run acrossed the road so as not to get run over. I made my way along a big piece of land that was empty, 'cause I could see the city on the other side.

Finally I found a fence where I could climb over, and I was rushing so fast that the fence got holt of my shirt and ripped it. But I didn't care right then. I ran straight out into the streets, not knowing where a hospital might be. First thing I seen was an alcoholic store, so I run in and there was a man there—a man from China or there-a-parts—who was watching TV and playing a crossword. There was a baseball game on the TV, but they warn't playing on account of the rain, and there was a big blue sheet covering most the entire field. I don't know why I remember a thing like that but I do, most like it was yesterday.

"Hey mister, where's the closest hospital?"

He warn't too happy to be disterrupted like that, but he looked up and pointed. "Six block that way," he says, talking fast. And I was off without saying goodbye. He was right too, and I found the hospital. But it was a tricky place for me to be, 'cause there's always policecops at a hospital, and other 'thorities too. I reckoned that I warn't as liable to be recognified if I warn't with Miguel, since they'd mostly be looking for the Mexigrant, but I didn't want to take too many chances with it. There was two policecops coming out of the door just as I was coming up—one of 'em was eating an apple and t'other one was laughing. I had to kind of sneak up on the doorway, and I hid down by the wheel of an ambulance.

Well I waited until they was out of the way, and I snuck in the door and went right up to the desk in the front, where there was a black lady who was dressed in blue and real fat like. I cleaned out my pockets and put all my coin money out on the table and even a couple of old bills that had been crumpled up good. I'll bet it was more than five dollars altogether.

"I need snake medicine," I says.

"Excuse me?" she says back to me, but she was distractified and didn't seem to pay good tension. "Have you been bit by a snake, honey?"

"Not for me. For my friend."

"Your friend's been bit by a snake?"

"A rattler. A biggun."

Well she was paying full tension now on account she seen the seriosity of the situation. "Your friend needs to come in to the hospital. Right away. You understand?" Well I 'splained that it warn't possible, so she started in on the questions. "Well, where is he? Is he at school? Is he with his parents?"

I finally just told her that he was a full-grown man. "So you need an ambulance?" she asks me.

"No ambulance. Just the medicine, okay? Is it enough money?"

She got real mad then, like I was hocusing her and not being serious. And I seen it warn't going nowheres. There warn't no way for me to 'splain why Miguel couldn't come without also 'splaining that he was a fugitive from the law. I shoulda taken more time to fix up some kind of a yarn before I come in to the hospital.

I malingered around for a bit and even made a dash down the hall after a time, thinking that's where they kept the snake medicine and maybe I could borrow a bit without them noticing. It was a desperation move you see, on account of Miguel being all alone and sick out there under the bridge, and I was worried what would happen to him if I didn't get the medicine or didn't get back fast enough.

But they had a guard there—kind of like a policecop but not official like—and he got me by the collar after somebody yelled, and he dragged me back out the door and threw me down on the ground like he thunk I was a troublemaker and not jus' trying to help a sick friend.

Well I was pretty sick to think that I had let old Miguel down and that we was in a heap of trouble now. I reckoned I should get back to him so he wouldn't be alone at least, but I warn't none too keen to show up without the snake medicine in my hand. It most breaked my heart to think what face Miguel would make when he seen it.

But there was a man there, who stopped me from going. He was leaning against a lamppost and smoking, and he had seen the guard throw me out on my bum.

"Excuse me, young man," he says to me, and he said it real political, like he was talking to a minister or a prince or some such, even though it was just me, Huck. He was wearing a suit and a tie, like somebody proper, but there was something about him that didn't seem proper. Like he was trying to pretend he was all regular and decent but it warn't so natural for him.

"I think you and I might be of some use to one another," he says, and he held out his hand for me to shake. "My friends call me the Duke."

You see, he'd been a-watching me, and he knowed what I was looking for. He took me around the corner and down a couple blocks to a real plain building that didn't have no signs outside. He said if I come along with him and did as he said then he'd make sure I got my snake medicine and maybe even some financial gains on top of that.

He licked his hand and tried to straighten out my hair before we went in there. "Now just play along, son, and I'll see if I can get you what you need." I didn't know what he was driving at exactly, but I reckoned that it was worth a chance at this point on account of Miguel's dire predictament. He told me that it wouldn't take no time at all, so I told him that we should get on with it, whatever it was.

Well the building was like a doctor's office, and we had to wait a while to see the doctor, but pretty soon he come in the little room and smiled real bright to see the Duke.

"Good to see you again, Mr. Duke." He was a short

little stumpy man and he was wearing a white lab coat. He didn't have but just a little bit of hair that was long and that he swirled around to try to cover his whole head.

"And you, doctor." They was talking too proper, like they was fancy people at a polo match or some such.

"I understand your son isn't feeling well, today." He looked at me.

"No, no. Not at all."

"I haven't met this one before. You certainly have a big family."

"Ah, yes. My wife and I sure do love the little children."

The doctor looked down at a form on his desk. "So you've got a tummy ache, son?" I decided to play along on account of my need for that snake medicine.

"Yessir," I says.

"Sounds like appendicitis. I'd like to operate immediately."

"But I—" That didn't sound right to me.

"It's okay, son," says the Duke. "The doctor knows best."

The doctor had me stick out my tongue so as he could push a stick in there and look around with a little flash-lamp.

"And you've got a sore throat, too?" the doctor asked me. But he still had the stick in there, so I couldn't answer. And that was bully by him, 'cause he warn't waiting for my answer, since he already had his own answer in his brain. He made to winker at the Duke. "When it rains, it pours."

"So to speak," says the Duke.

"Then you'll need a tonsillectomy too. And while we're at it a full battery of blood tests, X-rays, and urinalysis. It's a dangerous world we live in. You can't be too careful." He was trying to scare me now and doing a pretty good job of it. You see, it was clear to me that these was a couple of rapscallions that was up to no good. But it warn't clear to me what their game was and whether it involved real medical procedurals or just fake ones. I didn't want no surgery at that particular time, or maybe never.

"Now I just want to confirm. Your son does qualify for medical aid?"

"Just like all my other children," says the Duke. They got to taking a few pictures of my arms and legs and such just to make sure they had full documentration of my ailments. And I figured out quick that they didn't mean to cut me open. It was all just talk. Now you're prob'ly asking yourself why I would put myself in the hands of lowdown people like them that I didn't hardly know, but— as I 'splained before—I was in a dire predictament and was worried about Miguel. I knowed that I was making a mistake by associating with such lowdown humbugs and frauds. But I reckoned that the situation required me to make accommodations to my normal preferences. I warn't in a position to pick my friends just then.

At the end of it all, me and the Duke went outside and waited in the parking lot and I told him that I warn't sick at all. "Well, we all of us are in a state of part healthfulness and part sickness," he says. "I suppose it's just a matter of degree." And he lit up another cigarette but wouldn't give me one no matter how nice I asked.

He smoked a while and every now and again smiled at me like to make me jealous of how much he was enjoying it. And I was a-getting more and more worried about Miguel and impatient that the medicine would come before he got any sicker. But the Duke he had other thoughts on his brain. I noticed him taking the stock of me, like I was dog in the pound that wanted to come home with him.

"You've got moxy, kid."

"Thanks, Mr. Duke." I was being extra political on account of I still hadn't gotten that medicine yet.

"Not Mr. Duke. Just the Duke."

"Okay, Mr. the Duke."

He smiled then. "Where are your parents?"

"My mama went away a long time ago, and my Pap too I guess."

He was quiet for a time then, before he sprung it on me. He wanted me to throw my lot in with him, and together we could be rich. He said he needed a body like me, who could get people to warm up to him a bit, before he made to hocus them. He had an idea to recruit me into his rapscallion gang. Well, I told him that I warn't inclined to the rapscallion way, and that I warn't in favor of stealing money but just borrowing what I needed from time to time. He said that taking was taking, and my way was less profitable than his, so I was getting all the disadvantages of such activity—like I was going to hell just like him—without enjoying the full benefits thereof.

"I reckon I got too much of a conscience," I says to him. "So maybe I'll try not to borrow as much from now on." I told him that I couldn't help think about the people

I was borrowing from and how they might miss what I took. So he 'splained to me that's why it was better to steal from the gov'ment instead of regular folk, because then you wouldn't feel so lowdown on account of there warn't nobody with a face to think about. But he was hocusing me. Everybody knows the gov'ment ain't got no money of its own but only takes from the regular folk, so it warn't real what he was saying. Neitherways I didn't want to join no rapscallion gang, and I knowed that Miguel was prob'ly just about ready to die if I didn't get that medicine and get back to him soon enough. He was the only one in my gang for now.

Well finally we was disterrupted by a nurse lady who poked her head out the back door and handed the Duke an envelope. "Thanks, hun," he says, and then he took some bills out of the envelope and handed 'em to me directly.

"What's this?" I says. Money warn't no good to me then.

"Okay, okay. You can't blame a man for trying." He handed me a couple more bills. "Don't thank me. Thank your Uncle Sam."

"I told you. I don't want no money. I need medicine. Snake medicine." I was getting ornery with him now.

"That was for real? I thought you were just working some kind of angle."

I handed him the money back.

"You promised."

He considered this for a moment and then knocked on the back door again.

"You're lucky I'm an honest crook, kid."

Well after a bit the nurse lady come back with some snake medicine, like he promised, and she gave it to the Duke and I thought I was pretty near home free, and Miguel was a-gonna be so happy to see what I done, and proud of me for doing it too.

But then all of a sudden it seemed like the Duke struck an idea in his brain, and he didn't give the medicine to me straight away. "It suddenly occurs to me," he says. "Why would a healthy young man need antivenin so desperately?"

"Give it here," I says, and I tried to say it hard so he'd do what I wanted.

"And I'm starting to wonder why you look so awful familiar to me." He didn't hand over the medicine but tucked it into the pocket of his suit coat, and then he just walked right past me toward the street, like he was a-leaving and taking the medicine with him. I ran up behind him and grabbed him so he couldn't go. I thought I'd try to be nice about it.

"Hey Mr. Duke, I really need that medicine." Well he spun around real quick then and grabbed me. It had all been a trick. We was on the sidewalk now, right by one of them boxes where they put newspapers. That's what he'd been aiming for all along. He grabbed me by the back of my shirt and he pushed my face up close to the glass on the front of the newspaper box. My nose was even smushed up against it then.

"Why, lookkit that. A perfect match. I knew I'd seen you before." I was looking straight at a photogram of myself, right on the front page of the newspaper. "Why, Huckleberry, you should have mentioned that you are a celebrity."

The Duke was a-grinning, and it warn't a friendly smile no more, but a smile that said he had one over on me. And I knowed we was in real trouble now.

CHAPTER 18

I String the Duke Up and Leave Him Hanging on a Fence

THE Duke he got holt of my arm real tight, and he made me take him to Miguel. You might judge me for taking him there, but I figgered I didn't have no choice, and at least then it'd be two 'gainst one, if'n Miguel was still awake.

"Now the way I figure it, you weren't kidnapped like they say. You're on the lam." He was smart that Duke. Not in the normal way, but in a rapscallion way. By and by, he had most of it figgered out.

"Yeah, you're on the lam alright. Probably with this illegal stable boy. You hurt those ladies together?" Well I didn't take kindly to the incineration, and the Duke he seen it.

"No, I suppose not. But you are on the run with this illegal. And my guess is that somehow he got himself bitten by a snake. Is that right?" See, I told you. Rapscallion smart.

"I thought so," he says, 'cause he could see in my face that he'd hit on something near enough the truth. "Now this is how we're going to play it. You're gonna take me to this friend of yours, and I'm going to give him some of this medicine so that he doesn't die on us. And then I'm going to decide what angle I want to play."

It was reassuring to hear that he warn't gonna let Miguel die, but it didn't take a perfesser to see that our situation warn't gonna be real profitable with this fellow the Duke involved. So I made to tug myself away, but he kept a good lock on my arm. He was strong too. Rapscallion strong.

"Just let me go!" I says.

"Now why would I do that?" he asks me nice and easy, 'cause he knowed that he got the higher hand. "Everybody in the world is out looking for you. And I'm the only one that knows where you are." He smiled then but it was an oily grin with big ugly teeth. He was showing his true features now.

"It's gotta be worth something to somebody."

When I looked up at him, I could see the little package of antivenin hanging in his pocket. But there warn't no way to get at it from where I was at. But I'd struck an idea in my brain, and I was decided to try it out, since it might could be the best chance that me and Miguel could get free of the Duke. A lot of hours had passed by now, and Miguel prob'ly needed the medicine even more so than before.

We was getting closer now, so I took him down to the fence where I'd clumb over to get out of the river and go find the snake medicine. He let go of me so as I could climb up there to get over ahead of him. But he warned me as I done it.

"Now don't you think of running off, Huckleberry. Remember that I've got the medicine for your friend." He didn't have to remember it to me. I knowed it well and good. Well once I got up and over, the Duke started up. But he warn't none too clever or smooth about it.

So I tried to help him by telling him how to do it right.

"There's a place to put your toes right there," I says, and he follows my instruction. Well as he hoisted hisself up, his coat catched on a snaggly part of the fence. It was the same place where my shirt got ripped a couple hour before. You see, I done it for purpose. I showed him where to climb so as he'd get catched there. And here my plan had worked jus' about as good as I coulda 'magined.

Before he knowed it, I had jumped back up on the fence and I had a-holt of his suit, and I pulled down near as hard as I could so his jacket—the part they called the lapel—was full-on attached to the fence.

You shoulda seen what his face looked like then!

"You sonofa—!" He yelled at me and tried to swipe at me, but his hands was too big to go through the fence. I snuck my hand through one of them holes, though, and got holt of the snake medicine in his pocket and pulled it back through the other side. I'd done it!

I jumped down from the fence but not before I told him why I done it.

"We had a deal," I says, and it was the truth, and he knowed it. But you could see how angry it made him to be remembered of it in his immedious predictament.

"You sonofabitch!" He started using words that was some of my Pap's favorites. But it didn't scare me none, 'cause he was strung up on that fence. "You're going to regret this, Huckleberry!" But he was wrong. I ain't never regretted it all the way up to this current day.

I turned and run to find Miguel. I couldn't enjoy my hocus trick for too long, on account of Miguel being awful sick and I hoped not dead. I run back down to that bridge and found him right where I'd left him. He hadn't neither moved an inch. And he couldn't barely talk at all. I was jus' glad he warn't dead, 'cause he was the one true friend I had left in the world, 'cept Ben Rogers who was all the way back home and Tom Sawyer who was with his Aunt Polly.

Well I watched Miguel give hisself that shot. I never seen anybody braver. His hands was a-shaking, and there was sweat dripping all down his face. But he done it, and

pretty soon we was back on our raft. He warn't in any shape to talk or even set straight up. So he laid down and closed his eyes, and I got to navigating us down the river. I wanted to get as far aways from the Duke as I could get. He warn't no friend to us, and I knowed it.

CHAPTER 19

Miguel Sings
a Mexigrant Song

ONCE I got us out into the river, I set back down and took out my blade again. Miguel was still sleeping, so I started in on scratching some drawings onto the raft so as to mark it for me and Miguel. It warn't too long before my blade remembered me of my mama. That's how it is when you're doing something or making something with your hands—it gives your brain the room to meamble a bit and maybe remember or ruminate on other things.

I didn't have no clear pictures of my mama in my brain, on account she left and went away so long ago. But still you'd say that she made a big 'pression on me, 'cause I still had the feeling of her inside me. She was warm and kind and soft, not at all the type of woman you'd think would go along with a man like my Pap. Maybe that's why he took a liking to her. She warn't neither like to hit back or talk back, and she always looked for the good in a person even if it was hid pretty good behind bad stuff, like it was with Pap. He wouldn'ta said that he liked her so much now, but hated her instead for all she done to him. But hate usually gets it start as something else, then only turns to hate later.

I wondered to myself what my mama woulda said about all this stuff that had happened since I come to California. I know she'd be monstrous proud that I stood up to Jefe and got a reward for doing it. But now I was on the run from the 'thorities with an illegal Mexigrant. From one way of looking at it, it was a bully 'venture and I was lucky to be on the river with Miguel. And he hadn't done nuthin real wrong 'cept follow his parents and try to make a place for hisself in the world. But on t'other hand my mama was 'gainst me doing stuff that was illegal, and here I was aiding and abetting an illegal Mexigrant who was being chased by the policecops. I turned it over and over in my brain and couldn't neither get it straight.

There was a monstrous ghostful hooing just then, and I looked up to see an awful big owl looking down on us from from an electricity pole. But I couldn't see him right and clear, jus' his shadow against the sky, which was already beginning to get a little bit light. I know you think that Los Angeles is a big city and that's it just thousands and thousands of people and cars and sky-scratchers and no animals anywhere, 'cept the ones that people keep in their houses as slaves. But I'm here to tell you different. There's all sorts of critters running free and clear in Los Angeles, and some of 'em is just as wild as anything you'd see in the deepest darkest part of the woods back home in Missouri. I wouldn'ta believed it if I hadn't seen it myself.

Well Miguel was kind of stirring a bit, and he must've been feeling better because he started in on singing. And it was the most beautiful Mexigrant song you ever did hear.

> *Este es el corrido del caballo blanco*
> *que en un día domingo feliz arrancara*
> *iba con la mira de llegar al norte*
> *habiendo salido de Guadalajara.*
>
> *Su noble jinete le quitó la rienda,*
> *le quitó la silla y se fue puro pelo.*
> *Cruzó como rayo tierras Nayaritas*
> *entre cerros verdes y lo azul del cielo.*
>
> *A paso más lento, llegó hasta Esquinapa*
> *y por Culiacán ya se andaba quedando.*
> *Cuentan que en los Mochis, ya se iba cayendo*
> *que llevaba todo el hocico sangrando.*
>
> *Pero lo miraron pasar por Sonora*
> *y el valle del Yaqui le dio su ternura.*
> *Dicen que cojeaba de la pata izquierda*
> *y a pesar de todo, siguió su aventura.*

It was monstrous sad but beautiful too. It was all in Mexigrant so there warn't no meaning in it for me, 'cept it made me feel lonesome for Missouri, and I wondered if maybe Miguel was lonesome for Mexico, or at least for his family in Arizona. That's what a good song will do some-time—make you share a feeling with somebody else, even if you and him got totally different circumstantials.

By the end I warn't divided two ways about helping him no more. And if my mama was there to hear the song, she'da said the same thing. Besides, he'd saved me from my Pap who wanted to kill me, and my mama was prob'ly in favor of him on account of that.

I didn't say nuthin but just kept scratching in the wood on the raft. By the end, it said "Miguel and Huck." I put his name first because that's what you do for a friend. I'll

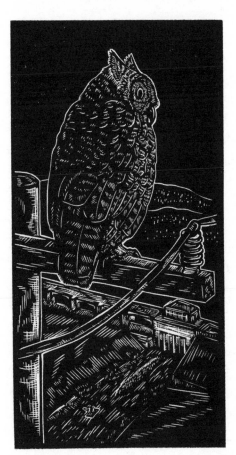

bet you woulda done it too if you woulda knowed him.

I figgered we had a clear path down the river and maybe a night or two more of floating 'til we come to Tom Sawyer and his Aunt Polly. It still warn't no more than a glimmer in my brain that she'd be able to help Miguel, but at least it'd be more than just me and him against all the 'thorities and policecops. But that strange river in Los Angeles warn't done with us yet.

CHAPTER 20

Pap Lays a Trap

ONCE we come out of the wooded area, we immediously come right up on a monstrous tall tower made out of concrete. Well it was a dam, and it was all closed up to watercraft, though the water seemed to be getting through alright. You wouldn't think there'd be a dam in the middle of Los Angeles like that, but it's the truth. I seen it myself. We most got run up into a whole pile of junk and garbage that had gotten the channel clogged up. I had to work hard to pull our little raft over to the side. Miguel he was still acuperating from being bitten by that rattlesnake. I left him there on the raft next to the river. He was awake but still not feeling very good about hisself.

I clumb up on the concrete and looked 'round and pretty soon I found a clear way where we could go up and around the dam and then get back down to where there was water on the other side. It warn't an easy way, though, and I knowed that me and Miguel would have a difficult time getting the raft over the other side.

"We gotta go up and over," I told him. I was a-pointing up to the top of the concrete, and from where we was it looked near a thousand feet tall.

"I can do it," Miguel says, "if you help me, Huck." That's just how he was. I never seen anybody stronger, without which it was my Pap when he had the rabies. Miguel he got up then, but it was hard. It took him a time to get hisself steady, and then we did it. We carried and dragged our homemade raft up that concrete wall and then down the other side. But then I realized that I hadn't scouted far enough. On the other side, the river went back to having straight up walls, and there warn't no way for us to get up over the fence and down to the water without getting ourselves injured on the concrete or busting up our raft.

From that side, we looked back at the dam, and we could see one spot where maybe we could get through if we worked at it. Miguel was moving slower and slower, but he agreed that we didn't have no choice but to go back the way we come. So we clumb back up over the dam, and it was hard on account it was overgrown with scraggly weeds everywhere. And when we made it to the top, we had to go back down the concrete part. Miguel fell once and made a noise that made me think he warn't feeling too well. But he got hisself back up, and 'ventually we got the raft back in the water.

Well the way the dam was built it had different skinny parts where water could pass through, most like car lanes on a road where they make you pay to go through. So me and Miguel we tried best we could to pick the right lane that gave us the best chance of making it to the other side. We got jammed up in there, on account there was so much branches and other such trash as gets stuck in a dam. Miguel didn't have the spunk of a rabbit, but he stayed real calm and told me what junk to move and how, so pretty soon we had a clear way, and the raft just sailed right on through.

It was sure a bully sight to look back and see that we'd made it past that dam that seemed like it warn't meant to be passed. Now we was in a narrow channel on the other side, with sides straight up like we'd seen from up above. The water was down a bit, 'cause it hadn't rained since yesterday. But it was still good for a raft and pretty soon we was floating down the river again. Right away we went under one of them Los Angeles freeways that sometime go fast but usually get all crammed up with cars. We could see 'em up there, and—even though the river warn't moving so swift anymore—we figgered that we was moving faster than those cars. They couldn't see us though, or more likely they didn't take the time and tension to do it, which is common in California. It was bully by me and Miguel, though, not to be noticed by nobody.

There was a long stretch now where the river tucked back behind some little houses. It was narrower here, and there was big plants growing on either side. It felt real peaceable and remembered me of a movie that Miss Watson had showed me. The movie was in a place where there was little canals running all through the city, and there warn't no cars but only boats that would take you from place to place, and a man would stand on the back of the boat and steer it where you wanted to go and even sing a

bully song for you. Well we didn't have no man to do it, so
I used my pole to steer, but from the front not the back.

We hadn't neither been on the river for much more
than a few miles yet, and already we seen places that looked
like a creek and other places that looked like a concrete
ditch and even other places that looked like a tunnel. And
of course there was the place where it seemed like a proper river winding through the woods and this place where
it was like a canal. And yet still we was mostly hidden,
and it seemed like most people warn't even knowledgeful
that there was a river at all and never woulda thought that
there was two fugitives floating right under their noses on
the way to the ocean.

After that the river got big again, more like a freeway
but down in the ground, only there warn't no cars and
only one raft. It went straight along with the real freeway,
and it was mostly all concrete again, with only an occa-
sional clump of trees and such. There was lots of birds
though, enjoying the water and pretending they warn't in
the middle of a city but maybe on a river or a lake in the
country. We even come up on a whole group of Canadia
geese that flew off when they seen us and did it in a V for-
mation like they always do. We passed right under a place
where they had horses—we could hear 'em a-braying—
and me and Miguel traded eyes and thought on Carolina
for a bit and hoped she was okay.

It was the middle of the day now, and it felt like we
was out in the open and maybe likely to be seen by some
policecops or somebody else who would tell the policecops. But nuthin never happened. We just floated. After a

while Miguel he said we oughta play it safer, so we pulled our raft over and hid in a little narrow channel that was cut in the concrete. It was a place where the water would come spilling in during a rainpour, but it was quiet now and the perfect place to hide a while. Miguel went back to sleep so as to get his gumpshun back, and I laid on my back and watched the clouds go by, just like I did that day down by the Salton Sea. A body could most forget that we was on the lam from the policecops and from my Pap too.

Well 'ventually I fell asleep like Miguel even though the sky was bright and wakeful. I waked up sometime around the middle of the afternoon and saw a couple of policecops up on the bridge that was a little ways down from us. But they was looking the other way and didn't neither pay tension to the river, supposing that there warn't nuthin or nobody down there. I'd been learned different by then, but I warn't inclined to let 'em in on the secret. Before you knowed it, they was gone, and I went back to sleeping.

Being on the run meant that me and Miguel was doing whatever regular folk wouldn't do. Regular folk would forget all about the river and never go down there, and we was using it as our escape route. Regular folk would sleep all night and get up in the morning, and we was sleeping during the day and then getting up after the sun went down. That's how it was this day too. After it come on dark, Miguel he waked me up and said it was time to go again. So we pushed out of that little channel that had been our home for most of the day and back out onto the river. The river was turning to the right now, a-curving around some mountains and turning south toward the ocean Miguel said.

We come under the freeway and that's when we got our first glimpse of the downtown part of Los Angeles. It was way off far away, but you could see a bunch of sky-scratchers right out in front of us, twinkling in the darkness and inviting us down to visit them. They looked small from where we was at, but I knowed that they'd get bigger and bigger the closer we got. Turning south meant we was turning toward my friend Tom Sawyer too, who lived past downtown a ways. I mentioned Aunt Polly the lawyer to Miguel again, but he didn't say nuthin back, prob'ly on account that he didn't want to get his hopes up.

It was smooth riding then, and there started to be trees and plants and critters again. I started to feel awful comfortable, thinking about the river back home and how any

place could be home if it had a proper river in it. You'da thought that maybe this river in Los Angeles warn't proper, but I had judged it proper by then, 'cause I'd seen myself how it could serve for a getaway and for a 'venture, and we'd met so many people and critters in just the couple of days we'd been a-living down there. There was electrical lines running this way and that over the river, strung between huge metal towers that looked like robot skeletons in the dark. We passed some rapids, and our little raft did okay and only got caught up a couple time.

But the smooth part warn't gonna last. As we come around a big bend, the river got real narrow, and the water was rushing so much we could hear the rapids. It was right near a big cement bridge, one of them real nice ones they got in California. We got ready for the rapids, but there warn't no moon that night, so it was hard to see what was coming. Well, what was coming was a trap.

We just barely saw it before we run straight into it. It was a stack of shopping cars piled in the narrow part of the river, so as we couldn't pass. The water made it through fine, but our raft didn't have nowheres to go, and so we pushed right up into the shopping cars. Well, he hadn't made his presence appreciated yet, but it was a trap that Pap had built, and a clever one too.

Because of the shopping cars, one end of the raft got a little higher than the other end, and pretty soon the lower end was taking on water, which made me and Miguel go overboard and straight into the river water. I was a-thrashing with my arms and feet, trying to find the bottom, but the river was deeper than normal there. Miguel he grabbed holt of my shirt and dragged me over to the shore, which was rocky and full of all such junk that had washed up from the river.

"Don't worry, *muchacho*," Miguel says atwixt his hard breathing. "I will go back and save our raft."

But he didn't get the chance, 'cause that's when I seen Pap. Actually the first thing I seen was the camper. A car passed over the bridge and its eyelamps passed over a dark spot by the side of the bridge and showed what was hiding there, which was the camper. I felt a jolt then, like I was hit by a lightning strike. I knowed we was in trouble, and right away I seen a dark shape a-scrambling down the cement wall. It was Pap, alright, just like you guessed. I couldn't see him too good from there, but I knowed it right away.

"It's Pap!" I yelled. And Miguel looked up just as we heard the pop-pop-pop of gunshots. Well we was lucky then, 'cause Miguel had dragged me over to the opposite side of the river from where Pap was a-hiding and a-waiting for us. And it was real dark, so he couldn't neither see us any better than we could see him. So he missed. But it ain't comfortable being out in the open with someone shooting shots at you, so Miguel he pulled me up quick and we made a dash for the trees that was growing on the shore at that part of the river. We heard a splash behind us when Pap crossed the river, and then he took a couple more shots but before you knowed it we was hidden good and well by the trees. It warn't easy going in the dark, and we could hear Pap behind us, a-ranting and a-raving as he crashed through the brush.

"Now you're done for, you slimy little toads! No more raft! We're on foot now, and only one of us got a gun."

Me and Miguel didn't make to respond, 'cause he was right about our predictament. Still, I got lots of practice running through the woods, and Miguel was finally feeling the full benefits of the snake medicine, so we was going just about as fast as we could. But Pap must've been sobered up, 'cause we could hear him behind us, and it didn't sound like we was pulling free from his pursual. Now and again, he'd yell out something mean and low-down, like how Miguel had fallen for his trap because he was a ignorant Mexigrant. He couldn't help hisself in that way. Even when he was trying to kill you, he wanted you to know that he didn't have a high 'pinion of you.

There was one spot where the woods opened up on our right and we could see the cement part that led up to the street. Me and Miguel stopped for a second to look. It was awful temptatious as an escape route, 'cause Pap would have a harder time shooting at us up on the street where there might be policecops or other people.

"C'mon," I says to Miguel. "We gotta get out of the river."

"Not here, Huck," says Miguel, and he points up there. "He will see us."

And I seen what he meant right away. The cement part was awful steep, and there was a monstrous tall fence at the top. There was even a street lamp up there that was giving off some light to see by. If Pap come up out of the woods and saw us up there, he'd have a clear shot. So I followed Miguel back into the woods, even though I was starting to feel exhaustered. I tried my best to keep up with Miguel, but I could tell he was holding back on account of me. And all the time Pap was behind us with the gun.

Well I'm not monstrous proud of it, but here's where I stumble tripped and busted my ankle good. I must've hollered, 'cause Miguel come back to me and tried to help me up. It was dark so I couldn't be sure, but I must've stepped on a rock or something and my ankle turned the way it warn't built to do. It happened to me once before when I was chasing a deer through the woods back home. It hurt something awful, just like it did the first time.

"C'mon Huck," Miguel says to me. "We've got to keep going." He lifted me up but I couldn't barely walk no more but just hobble. And Pap must've heard me too, 'cause now he was a-cackling and a-calling out from the dark.

"Now I've got you!" he says. "You're hurt now, aren't you? Well I'm a-comin' and I'm a-gonna fix both of you once and for good!"

Miguel took me on his back then. You'd never've thought he could do it, if you'd a seen him after he got bit by the snake. But he'd found his strength again. He ran and ran, and I knowed I was slowing him down, 'cause I could hear Pap getting a little bit nearer all the time, on account of he was alone and didn't have to carry nobody on his back.

Well we was prob'ly done for, but Miguel just wouldn't stop, and I kept holt of him the best I could. It started so's we could hear Pap breathing hard so we knowed he was a-closing in on us, and I started in to feeling bad for Miguel that he'd gotten mixed up with such folk as me and my Pap. It warn't right that he was bound to get hisself shot and killed just for being a good friend to me and saving my life. And I started to think maybe I could get free of Miguel, so as Pap would have to kill only one of us and not both, and he'd prob'ly pick me, on account of I was his bloodson. It was a lowdown thought, and I didn't want to do it neither, but sometime there ain't no choices available but bad ones.

And then—just like that, just as I was a-making up my brain to jump free of Miguel—we come out of the woods and into a sort of a clearing. There was dozens of tents, red and green and blue, all around. Well we was out of tree cover to protect us, and Pap was coming up fast behind, so Miguel just kept going, a-weaving in and around all those tents. The sun was coming up a little bit now, so there was a little bit of light, which warn't in our favor, since now Pap would have an easier time of aiming his gun at us. But then Miguel crashed right into a fellow who was up real early, and we all went down in a pile on the ground. And right away we heard Pap laughing.

Here he comes, 'merging from the woods with the gun in his hand and walking straight toward us. It seemed we was done for, but then the fellow that Miguel ran into seen Pap and kind of figgered out what was going on. He put his fingers in his mouth and made just about the loudest whistle you ever heard without which it was from a train. Pap was coming up, but pretty soon the whistle done its work and all sorts of people started waking up and coming out of their tents to see what the kermotion was about. Afore you knowed it, we was surrounded by all sorts of people who looked like they'd been camping down there for a week or maybe more. And they was right atwixt us and Pap. He stopped then, and the 'spression on his face changed from a kind of smile to a kind of a scowl, but still showed the rabies in his eyes. Even he knowed he couldn't well shoot all those people with only just his gun.

"This ain't finished," he says. And he was talking straight to me and maybe Miguel too. He had his eyes fixed on us the whole time and it was most like he barely even saw all them other people. Then he went and disappeared back into the woods.

CHAPTER 21

Taken in
by Some Actervists

WHEN Pap disappeared, all them people turned to look at us. And it was a rabbleshackle group if I ever seen one. I figgered 'em right away for my kind of folk, 'cause they was camping down by the river just like I done back home. Most of these people was real dirty too, like they warn't inclined to take a bath, and some of 'em had drawings on their skin but more pretty than what Ivan had. And some of 'em even had metal things a-hanging off of their faces. It didn't bother me none, 'cept I wondered how much it hurt.

They was real welcoming and got into fixing us some breakfast when they realized how hungry we was. They had bacon and eggs and beans too, and I couldn't hardly remember a time when a breakfast tasted so good. I seen Miguel, and I could tell he was a-savoring the victuals just like me. Them people didn't ask too many questions neither, which was bully by me and Miguel. There was Worker Alexis and Worker Joshua and Worker Nicholas. Nicholas was the one Miguel had collissioned with when we run into their camp. There was even a fellow with a guitar who called hisself Worker Dandelion, though I never heard of a man called after a flower before then. Every one of 'em had Worker at the front of their name, and so Miguel asked what line of work they was in. But they said they warn't workers yet but just students in a real fancy college where they let the weeds grow all over the buildings on account they was too busy reading dusty old books to trim 'em back. Anyway, they warn't inclined to work in the current situation 'cause there was money in it. They said they would be more inclined to work in a situation where there warn't no money in it. And that's what they was waiting and hoping for somewheres down the line.

The main topic of conversating at breakfast was how rich a person could get to be before he couldn't be a good person no more. Worker Joshua said that most everybody in the world was good and true, 'cept maybe ten percent of the people, and them was the richest. But Worker Nicholas—he was the one with a bully red beard—said that you couldn't have no money at all or else you was as good as damned to hell for the rest of eternality. And it was better to give away all your money and quit your job for good. Well, a bunch of the folk agreed with that, but one girl, Worker Alexis, raised her hand and said that she didn't think that was so, 'cause there was lots of folks with jobs who was good people, like her aunt who was a schoolteacher. So the bearded fellow cut it back a bit and said that it was prob'ly about half of the people who was good and half that was bad, and the half that was bad was the rich half.

Well then the girl said that her other uncle was a doctor, and she figgered that he was prob'ly in the upper half but he never done no harm to nobody but was always trying to help 'em. And so they revised their thinking again and decided that anybody who was richer than a doctor was lowdown and evil for sure, until another one of 'em said that he had a friend who had a lot more money than a doctor but was always giving it away, and, after a discussion, everyone agreed that this fellow's friend couldn't be so evil and lowdown.

So they got to going 'round and 'round, taking a survey in a way and figgered out that none of 'em knowed anybody that made more than a million trillion dollar every year. So they decided that was the proper cut-off, and everybody below that was good, and everybody above it was the worst kind of person who was 'sponsible for all the trouble in the world. Well that satisfied everybody well and good. I was thinking on my friend Buck Grangerford and wondering whether he fell on one side of their line or t'other. But I decided it didn't matter none, 'cause if they knowed him they could just adjusticate their line to accommodate him and his sisters. In the meanwhile, their conversating moved on to other intellectuous topics such as could a woman ever be as lowdown and evil as a man and whether the gov'ment should make everything free or jus' most stuff.

After breakfast Worker Nicholas took us over to one tent that was bigger than all the rest. It was as bully a teepee as I ever seen. And he 'troduced us to a fellow who called hisself Worker Brian. He set us down in his tent and gave us a kind of hot drink that smelled funny and told us all about the people there. He said they was all actervists, and they was just one tiny part of something wonderful called the Movement, which was bound to turn the whole world into a place where everybody was peaceable and equal and there warn't no more guns or money or other such stuff as gets people into trouble. He was their leader in a way, but they warn't inclined to have any leaders and instead all be equal, so we warn't allowed to call him the leader without which there was nobody else around.

"That sounds awful bully," I told him. "My name is Huckleberry."

"I know who you are," he says to us. "I've been following the story on the news the past couple of days."

"So you know we're on the wrong side of the law?"

"As far as I'm concerned, you're on the right side of the law. Because when the law is wrong, then the only right side is the wrong one." Well I was confuzzled by his words, but it sounded like we warn't in no danger of being handed over to the 'thorities. "You've been oppressed by the system, as far as I can tell," he says. "And we're going to do everything we can to help you."

Me and Miguel we traded eyes right then, and I could see that he was happy just like I was that we had gotten lucky and fallen in with such nice people who was inclined to help us.

CHAPTER 22

Me and Miguel
Most Get Mixed Up
in a Rebelution

NOW these people from the Movement was on the wrong side of the law too on account of they was generally against the policecops, but nobody was a-bothering 'em down there in the river, 'cept a couple of policecops who would walk around the outside of their camp a couple times a day. This Worker Brian fellow said it wouldn't be no problem for us to stay inside the tents and never be seen by nobody outside the Movement.

He said he had a plan whereas me and Miguel could be freed up from our predictament and Miguel would get to be with his family. Miguel tried to get him to tell it right then, but Worker Brian said it was still a-taking shape in his brain and that we needed to get started with the preparatories. Me and Miguel decided that we could wait and see what this fellow was thinking afore we made up our brains what to do next.

Brian borrowed me a dress from Worker Alexis—she was small like me—so that he could take me out of the camp and into town with him. He said that it was too dangerous for Miguel to come but he thought he could get me by the policecops okay, and that's how it worked out with the help of a big hat that blocked most of my face. Worker Brian had a real shiny car that come all the way from Eurasia, and I supposed that he had stolen it from somebody on account of he was so monstrous proud of not having no money. But he said that he got it as a real nice birthday present from his mama and papa, and it come just in time too, just a couple of weeks before he disowned 'em on account they was dirty rotten capitulists.

He took me to a shop where they had all kind of things you'd have in your house, and we started collecting all the supplies for the camp. It was monstrous uncomfortable in that dress and hat, but nobody paid me no tension. That's how it is in California. There's so many things to see and so many different flavors of people, that you can dress like a girl and no one would notice in a million year. It's not like Missouri where sometime they get all worked up about how you talk or dress and whether it's proper like or not. And this is one place where California got the better of it, by my way of thinking, 'cause then nobody's neither gonna bother me about being Huck.

In the meanwhile of us shopping, Worker Brian told a little bit about his plan. You see, there was this fellow coming into town the next day, a famous pollertician, and he was a bad one too, the worst kind in all the world. It was that same fellow we had heard on the radio when we was a-visiting with the Colonel, that fellow who called hisself Buck Harkness. And he was gonna speechify about all the bad the Mexigrants done. Well the plan was that we was a-gonna go and make a ruckus so as to disterrupt his speech and make it hard for anybody to hear him. I didn't understand how that was gonna help me and Miguel, but Brian said he was a-turning it over in his brain.

Worker Brian 'splained to me how there was two kinds of folks in the world—those that wanted to hurt other people and those that didn't. And this fellow Harkness, he and his followers was the first kind, which was also the worst kind. And the Movement was made up of the second kind of person, which is the best kind. I followed him over to the part of the store that sold rocks and wood and other such stuff as you can build other stuff with.

He picked up a big gray rock and made to throw it, but only just pretended. "This one's perfect!" he says, and he smiled real big when he said it. Worker Brian started stacking his shopping car with stones and rocks, so I helped him do it. He said if we throwed enough rocks at them people and called them real bad names, then maybe they'd see how they was wrong and pretty soon there'd be a new kind of world where everybody would listen to each other and be nice all the time, instead of trying to hurt one t'other. He said a bunch of other intellectuous stuff about communabilism and capitulism, but I got lost in the mumble jungle.

When we got back to camp with all them rocks, they already had dinner going, and Worker Brian called a meeting to tell us all what kind of plan he'd worked up. He took out some drawings that showed the place where this fellow Harkness was gonna give his speech. It was a kind of an outdoor theater. His plan was for most of the Movement group to get up close to the stage, and each of 'em would be hiding a rock in their clothes somewheres. In the meanwhile, Worker Brian would sneak me and Miguel in there 'round back with a couple of bully disguises. At the right time, the Movement folks would start a-throwing their rocks and a-yelling and a-screaming. His thinking was that they could create enough of a disturberance that the folks in the crowd would show their true flavors and start in with throwing rocks back. And then we could rush up on the stage and take this fellow Harkness as a kind of hostager.

It sounded to me like a proper kidnapping like a pirate would do, but Worker Brian said it was something called a provoccupation, which was better than kidnapping. Miguel he'd come out of all of it as a hero and a symbol, and not just a Mexigrant no more. Miguel he said that he didn't have no interest in being a symbol but just wanted to be with his family. But Worker Brian gave a bully speech about how it warn't right for Miguel to be shortsighted about it, seeing as how the rebelution was all about helping the lowdown Mexigrants in the world.

Well it sounded like a bully plan to me, but Worker Alexis kept asking questions and you could tell that she didn't think it was gonna work too well. Worker Brian said that she was wrong and that it was a bully way to get people everywheres to know more about the Movement and how peaceable they all was. After dinner, I tried to talk to Miguel about it, but he wouldn't say much. I decided that he was just nervous on account of what we was gonna do the next day and how he would most likely be free by tomorrow night. We went to sleep in one of the smaller tents, where they had made some room for us to lay down with some sleeping bags and a dirty old sofa cushion for a pillow.

Well I couldn't fall asleep right away on account I was excited to see what tomorrow would bring to us and whether me and Miguel might end up free. Worker Brian was wakeful too, so I started in on telling him my whole 'venture since I'd gotten to California. He'd read about me and Tom Sawyer and the busted-up drug deal on his computer and he'd formed all sorts of 'pinions based on that.

Right off he told me that I'd better pollergize to Tom, on account of I was white and he was black, and my granddad had been mean and lowdown to his granddad. He said that the black folk was lowdown and 'ppressed and they sure didn't have no chance at being happy or getting anywheres in the world. He said that it was because he loved them so much that he thought so. He said that I was prob'ly 'sploiting Tom whether I meant to or not.

I told him that me and Tom Sawyer was real good friends and I didn't think I was 'sploiting him and that Tom seemed like he was pretty happy with his lot. Well, he 'splained to me that Tom was lowdown and 'ppressed whether he knowed he was or not. The best way for me to be a friend to him was to watch real careful what I was saying all the time, so as I could avoid saying something racialist. He said it was dead wrong to talk free and loose with Tom Sawyer like you might with a regular friend. Well it didn't seem right to me, but I tried to have an opening in my brain about it, since I was still trying to make my way in this new place.

Worker Brian said that there was a magical place where they'd most got rid of racialism altogether. It was a place called Sanforcisco and it was more bully even than Los Angeles on account that all the people was the most lovingest people on the face of the earth. It sounded like a real bully place if you was black or a Mexigrant, but Brian said that none of 'em lived there no more. It was better that way too, he said, 'cause there warn't no chance that you'd run into one of 'em on the street and then say something racialist on accident.

After a time all that intellectuous talk tuckered me full out, and I fell asleep.

CHAPTER 23

A Midnight Escape!

I waked up and tried to scream, but I couldn't on account there was a hand a-clamped right over my mouth. Well I figgered right away it was Pap, and he'd done found us. But sometime you don't know what you think you know. After just a blink, I seen that it was *Miguel* and not Pap at all, and Miguel was making the sign for me to be quiet and not scream. So I didn't scream and instead followed Miguel out of the tent, real quiet like, so as not to wake up Worker Brian who was right there next to us. I wanted to ask Miguel what we was a-doing and why we was sneaking around, but he warn't in the mood to talk right then. So I followed him around the tents and we started making our way back upriver, where Pap chased us, which was the *wrong* way as far as I was consternated. But Miguel was my one true friend right then so I just followed along and decided that he would tell me his reasonings when he was ready.

After a time we come out of the trees and back to the place where Pap shot at us. Worker Alexis was there, and

she didn't act surprised at all to see us but instead immediously took us to the water. You won't believe it but our
raft was there! See, Miguel and Alexis had been at work
saving it from the shopping car dam that Pap had built, and
now it was back on the water on the other side. And I seen
right away that Miguel and me was gonna get back on the
raft and get back on the river and forget about Worker
Brian's plan. You see, Alexis had made out to help Miguel,
on account she had heard Worker Brian tell one of them
other workers that most likely we'd all get arrested and
none of us would be free, including Miguel, and that Miguel would most likely get shipped back to Mexico after
it happened. Brian said it was worth it though, on account
they needed to get some tension for the Movement so that
the rebelution would happen on schedule. Alexis thought
that it was a mean and lowdown thing to say, so right then
she made up her brain to help us escape back to the river,
so maybe we'd have some chance of getting Miguel free,
though she warn't sure it was possible even then.

Miguel was mighty thankful, and so was I when I
learned how Worker Brian was trying to hocus us. She
gave us both a hug, and we pushed off. Afore you knowed
it, we was floating down the dark just like before, and it
was a mighty warm feeling to be back on the river with
Miguel. For a time we could see the shadow of Alexis
a-waving to us from the shore, until we went 'round a
bend. We passed right by all those tents on the side of
the river, but all them Movement people was still asleep,
prob'ly dreaming about how bully things would be after the rebelution happened and people like them was in

charge. Maybe a part of me felt dismal and lowdown about missing out on the rebelution, but another part of me said that it warn't likely to happen the way them people thought. They had some awful nice ideas, but just because an idea's nice don't make it a true necessity. And usually it's the nice ones that get you into trouble, on account you ain't inclined to let 'em go quick enough. That's how it was with me when I thought that maybe Pap would make for a proper father.

This part of the river was wild again, and there was all kind of critters out in the middle of the night. Me and Miguel was real quiet then, so they warn't afeard of us. We saw a whole family of coons washing their paws in the water. And there was a funny little bird hiding back in the bushes on the side of the river. The top of his head was black, most like a top hat. But he didn't bother us none.

We could only see him on account we was near a bridge that had some lights on the top that was shining down and gave us a little light to see for a time. After we passed, it was awful quiet, and you'da never knowed that we was in the city. I heard a funny kind of a dog bark, and then a howling. It warn't too near, but it warn't that far neither. Pretty soon there was a couple more barks, and then come all such barking and howling as you can imagine, and some screeching too. It was such a kermotion it most gave me the fantods.

"*Coyotes*," Miguel says, and he says it in the Mexigrant way. "They are hunting."

"What do they hunt for?" I asked him.

"Maybe a cat. *Un gato*." That was Mexigrant talk for what regular folks call a cat.

Well they went quiet again, and me and Miguel supposed that the cat was dead by then. We stayed quiet a while on account we was feeling lowdown for the cat. We was being hunted too, and it warn't hard to think that maybe we'd end up as dead as that cat, if Pap ever got holt of us again.

We didn't get too far before Miguel wanted to hole up again. We found a pipe that was covered with a big red metal lid. Somebody had done painted eyes and a nose and even whiskers on the lid, so as it looked like a cartoon cat. The lid was real heavy, but Miguel he was able to get it open, and so we went in there before the sun come up. After everything that had happened we was so tired that it seemed natural to go to bed at the wrong time. And after we crawled into the pipe, Miguel let the lid back down again, so it was plenty dark. It was a strange place for a bed, but me and Miguel warn't too particular. So we laid right down in the curve of the concrete, and I tried to hope that there warn't nobody living a little further up in the dark. The other thing I hoped for was that there wouldn't be a surprise rainpour that would send water crashing down on us from the street. It warn't too stormy right then, but I knowed that we was in the path of the water, if it ever come.

Miguel must've had some sort of a clock in his brain that day, 'cause he waked me up just as it was coming dark again. He said it was time to go, and he already had the big metal lid open. There was just a little bit of light left from the sun which was down behind the mountains, and that little light was yellow and orange, just like you'd 'magine at a time like that. It made the river look warm and comfortable for a couple of fugitives like us.

I used my pole to push the raft out into the stream. By this time it was most full dark again. For a time we was quiet, and we listened to the sounds of the river and the sounds of the city, which kind of mixed up with each other in a way that made a body feel everything might come good in the end. It was a false feeling in a way, 'cause there's no way to know how a thing's gonna end when you're in the middle of it. A little later it starts to seem like there warn't no other way for things to go but turn out the way they did. But that's only later. When you're there, you can't know for sure but jus' do the best you can. Me and Miguel both knowed it then. And I still know it now.

We passed under another bridge and there was a

ghostful sound coming from under there. It was just pi-geons a-course, but we couldn't see them on account they was tucked up in the nooks and craters of the bridge. Well their coo-cooing made it seem like that bridge was haunt-ed, and it was one more thing that made the river magic like. I was happy when we passed through okay and it got all quiet again.

But it warn't full quiet for long. We 'ventually come up 'round a bend in the river, and we started to hear some kind of sound, most like drums or some such. Well it was full dark by that time, so it didn't seem right, but the closer we got the louder the drumming got, and it sounded like a song that was fit for a bunch of cannibals afore a feast. We could see a fire through the trees, and whiskers of smoke was a-curling up toward the stars.

CHAPTER 24

The Strangest Kind
of Church You Ever Seen

SOMEBODY yelled out a "Whoop!" as we come nearer. And then someone else yelled "Allelujah!" There was a whole bunch of folk gathered 'round a fire that was as tall as two men and as wide 'round as I'd ever seen a fire before. They was dancing 'round and 'round the fire a-whooping and a-yelling out their allelujahs. Well it was a fantastic sight and not like anything I never seen before. After a time, the group started in on singing together, only it warn't quite proper singing but more like a chantsong. But it still had considerable power.

> *Awake, O sleeper, rise up from the dead,*
> *And Christ will give you light!*
> *Awake, O sleeper, rise up from the dead,*
> *And Christ will give you light!*

They sang it over and again, and all the while they was dancing.

Now one of them dancers seen us and our raft

approaching, and she took herself out of the line and come over to the shore to greet us in a way. And I steered the raft over toward her on account I warn't scared but more wondering what this was. We hadn't barely made any progress yet, but Miguel didn't say nuthin when I started angling over. I guess he had a good bit of curiopathy, just like I did. With the firelight a-flickering on her face, that young girl looked near on an angel, and her voice was like an angel too.

"Hi there," was all she says at first. She didn't have no shoes on, which gave me a good feeling about her right away, and she had a dress on that had little yellow flowers all over it. She was prettier than anything I ever seen in California or Missouri. You'd say the same thing if you was there too. She most looked like a magical fairy, 'specially with the firelights dancing on her face and making it all glowful.

"What is this?" Miguel asked her. "What is going on here?"

"We are the Flock. Welcome to our church."

"This ain't like no church I ever seen," I says to her.

Well she smiled then and looked around. First at the fire, then at the river a-trickling down to the ocean, and then up at the stars a-twinkling down on us. Finally she come back down to look at me and Miguel, and her look was warm and full of good feelings.

"Is this not the House of God?"

Well Miguel he smiled then, and he stepped off the raft. I did too.

"My name is MaryAnn," she says. "Would you like to break bread with us?"

The dancing kept going on for a whiles, but by and by
everybody stopped dancing and went a little ways down
from the fire where there was blankets on the ground.
Everybody come forward, one by one, and put food down
on the middle blanket, and pretty soon there was so much
food you coulda fed the whole town of St. Petersburg, if'n
they was hungry in the middle of the night.

The whole group of 'em had been fasting, MaryAnn
says, so they was most starved, but it warn't right to eat
until the food was blessed. There was a woman there who
was taller than every other person there, even the menfolk.
She stepped into the middle just then, and every person
there went quiet and paid their full tension to her.

"That's Sister Abigail," MaryAnn whispers to me, and
she smiled when she said it.

Sister Abigail warn't like any other person I'd ever
seen in my life. Like I was saying, she was as tall as a
person could be without bumping her head on the sky.
We was sitting right there under her, and I had to look
straight up to see her face, most like I was looking up to
a giant. And most of her head was shaved all off, 'cept for
a stripe right down the middle which was painted bright
red. And she had big round things that was in her ears,
so as you could see straight through her ear lobe if you
really wanted to. She had muscles too, most like she was
a man, but they looked good on her and showed how
strong she was. Her eyes was all dark, and it seemed like
maybe they'd been painted too. And her voice was loud
and strong, and it was the only thing we could hear, 'cept
the dribble-drabble of the river nearby.

"Beautiful people," she says, and she gave a stop here for a minute, before she kept going. "Thank you for gathering here on this magical night when we celebrate the coming resurrection of our Lord. We thank the Great Mother above for looking down upon us and holding back the rain so that we might worship out under Her sky."

I'm not one who likes religious speechifying, but this was as good a talk as ever I heard. Sister Abigail held up her hand, and there was a loaf of bread in it.

"As we share this bread, let us reflect on the night that the apostles gathered together for dinner under the stars, the night before the Christ was killed. Let us remember the sacrifice that He made for us all, and let us strive to live up to His standards of love and selflessness."

She tore off a piece of bread and ate it then, before she bent down and handed the loaf to MaryAnn. "The body of Christ," says she to MaryAnn, and MaryAnn took the bread and done the same thing. She turned to me and gave me the loaf. Well I warn't accustomated to it yet, so I just tore off a little piece and handed it to Miguel. Miguel he did it proper and said "the body of Christ" when he passed it to a skinny fellow who was sitting nearby with a funny little dog that had a scrunched-up face.

As I was chewing, Sister Abigail come over to me and Miguel and put her hands on our heads, first one and then the other. "Welcome, my sons," she says. "May God be with you." And then she went on making her way through the whole lot of people, touching 'em and saying kind words. She warn't like no preacher I ever seen, but—if I had to have a preacher—I'd have one like her. I'll bet you'd say the same if you knowed her.

We had a good meal then, and MaryAnn 'troduced us to all such people as was there, which was all different kinds. You wouldn't think so, but it most felt natural to have a meal like that in the middle of the night with a bunch of strangers a body had never met before. They was like a family and took care of each other like a family would. And me and Miguel we was like surprise dinner guests that was made to feel welcome even though nobody'd never invited us. We had all such truck as you'd ever want at a picnic, like mangoes and sandwiches and even cookies with cinnamon on 'em. There was songs too, some of 'em old and familial and other ones that I'd never heard before. But they was all the best kind of songs that would make a body feel good inside and all together with other people, not dreadful lonesome like you feel sometime when you're not singing.

After dinner MaryAnn took us over to another bridge that crossed the river. Sister Abigail was sitting back there, all alone, with her eyes closed as if she was thinking real hard about something, 'cept she was all relaxified. Behind her on the cement part of the bridge, they'd made a cross of sorts with two pieces of old wood that had come from the river. It warn't pretty but there was something about it that seemed right and good. MaryAnn brung us up right in front of Sister Abigail, who opened up her eyes to look at us. And we set down right there in front of her. There was candles all 'round that gave us a little bit of light to see and made it seem like a special place, not just regular.

"Sister Abigail, the Lord be with you," says MaryAnn.
"I want you to meet these travelers whom God has led to us."

"Yes, thank you MaryAnn," says the Sister. "Welcome my friends. What are your names?"

"I'm Huckleberry," says I. "And this is Miguel. We're traveling down this river."

"Thank you for sharing your food with us," says Miguel.

"We are always happy to have—." But she didn't have a chance to finish what she was a-gonna say. There was a ruckus from behind us, and we saw a man being held back by MaryAnn.

"They are fugitives!" he screamed. "That man is wanted for *murder*."

Me and Miguel traded eyes right then. We knowed we was in trouble. Again. Just then this fellow breaked free from MaryAnn and come right up to the Sister.

"Sister, there is *evil* in our midst!"

But MaryAnn was right behind him, and she was advercating for us as best she could.

"They are not evil," she says to this fellow and the Sister. "I feel the goodness in them." And she grabbed our hands then, prob'ly to show this fellow that she was on our side in a way.

The fellow—his name was Derek—was all red in his face, and he was a-breathing real hard, most like he was scared of us or some such. "This boy has been *kidnapped*, Sister. We must save him." I didn't know how to tell him the truth of the matters.

By now the rest of them people in the Flock had

heard the kermotion and was gathering all 'round, and me
and Miguel was feeling hemmed in again, like there warn't
nowheres to run if we made up our brains to leave.

Sister Abigail got up then and she come up close to
me, so as I felt about as small as an ant. Then she bent
down and got real low, so that her face was just about even
with me. I could see up close her red hair and the holes in
her ears and the paintings on her face. "Tell me the truth,
son." She said it real quiet, most like a whisper so nobody
else could hear. "Do you travel with this man of your own
free will? Has he done you any harm?"

"He didn't do nuthin wrong," I says. Here was my
chance to tell the truth about Miguel. "It was my Pap. I
swear it warn't Miguel. We're on the run on account of his
being illegal."

She looked at me straight then and didn't say nuthin
for a long while. Then she nodded.

"Thank you, son."

Then she stood up and made herself big again and her
voice loud again. Everybody was listening now, especially
me and Miguel.

"We should all thank Brother Derek for his vigilance in
protecting the community of God." Derek puffed up then,
just a little but I seen it, as he was feeling monstrous proud.

And she kept going. "But MaryAnn is right. These travelers have love in their hearts, and they deserve our prayer."

Derek yelled out then and made to disterrupt her. But
she held her hand up high, and he stopped right away
when he seen that. It warn't fear exactly, but she warn't
one to be disterrupted. After a second, Abigail started

talking again. "What man deems illegal, God may deem to be right and good and just." Well that took the tuck right out of Brother Derek, and he turned a bit more peaceable, which you could see in his face.

She put her hand on my head then, and I got the shivers in my back.

"I invite you to pray with me." When she said it, they all come forward—all of 'em—and they made a real tight ring around me and Miguel, and every one of 'em was touching me with their hands, or otherwise they was touching each other, most like we was all connected together. I was mighty uncomfortable, but I seen Miguel fall down so as he was standing on his knees, and he closed his eyes and put his head down, like he was a-praying.

In the middle there was still the Sister. "Great Mother, see to the safety of these travelers whom you have brought to our Flock. Protect them from the prejudices and the hatred of men."

Well, you can blame me for it, but you warn't stuck in the middle like I was, all crowded in. I squeezed myself free and then squirmed all the way through all them people's legs until I come out the edge of that big circle.

It didn't stop Sister Abigail, though. I couldn't see her no more but could hear her voice a-praying from the middle of the crowd. "And protect them from this government that sees fit to break the family ties that bind people together in love. We ask this in Jesus's name."

And then everybody said "Amen" all together.

It was a bully prayer, but I ain't one to be cramped in like that.

After the prayer, we went back to our raft, 'cause Miguel was feeling like we had to keep going and meet our fates somewheres down the river. They all waved g'bye to us as we floated away, but MaryAnn was at the front. She even gave us a kiss for each of us before we stepped back on the raft. She was full of beauty and goodness too, that MaryAnn.

CHAPTER 25

Explosives in the Sky

WE floated in the quiet for a time. I guess both of us was thinking about what had happened and the powerful bully prayer that the Sister had prayed for us. It didn't seem right to say words right then that would only jus' spoil the feelings. At least I thought so and from Miguel being quiet I thought maybe he had struck the same idea without saying so.

We was running along a freeway again, but this time headed south. It was later in the evening though, so there warn't as many cars on neither side. I had the feeling we was finally coming up on all them skyscratchers, but they was full hidden by a mountain that overloomed the freeway. We saw a policecop go by on his motorcycle, and he had his lights a-flashing and his siren a-blaring so as to chase somebody, but we couldn't see who he was chasing. Pretty soon a few more policecops come by, and the air was full of crying sounds, the kind that come from a policecop car. I wondered if maybe they'd found Pap and figgered out that he was the one to blame for all these troubles. Maybe they'd find him and arrest him, and they'd make him tell the truth, and then me and Miguel would be able to go back to Ms. Douglas's house with the horses. I thought about Ms. Douglas and Miss Watson then, and I wondered if they was dead or just hurt real bad. I hoped for the second one, but there warn't neither no way to know for sure.

I warn't accustomated to praying, and Pap said that there warn't no God at all, at least none that would look out for people like us. But I tried to make a prayer for them ladies then, and I told God just what I told you. That those ladies was good ladies and had been kind to me and that they didn't deserve to die or get hurt from a lowdown person like Pap. I told God that I wished that they would not be dead and get better and that one day I might be able to say thank you to them. I don't know if he heard me but I done it just the same.

They was the best kind of people, and it was on account of me that they'd got theyselves hurt by Pap. I got to feeling lowdown about it. Pap was my bloodfather and I figgered there warn't no way to get rid of him for good. Even if he was dead and gone, he'd still be in my dreams, a-whupping me and telling me I's no good. Well, it was dreadful lonesome to think about it that way, but I knowed it was full true, and there ain't no use a-hiding from the truth.

Still I thought on all the 'ventures I had and how my friends had been good and true and helped me 'scape my Pap when I could. There was Ben Rogers who brung food to my lean-to, and Tom Sawyer who helped me bust up Pap's criminality scheme. And Ms. Douglas and Miss Watson who'd taken me into their house and given me a place to be safe from Pap, at least for a time.

And Miguel was the best of 'em all. He'd saved my life, and I'd saved his life, and that was the surest way to know that you was true friends with a person. I was thinking all of this while I looked up at the stars. There warn't no diamonds a-hanging down, but they was beautiful just the same. Miguel he was looking up at the stars too.

So I jus' asked him. "You reckon there really is a God up there, looking down on us?"

"I don't know about up there," Miguel says. "But He is here, *muchacho*." And he touched his heart. "God is the good that is inside of all of us. That is what I believe."

"My Pap says God done forgot about us Finns a long time ago. We're on our own."

"I think no, Huck. Think about the people we've met on the river and how many of them have helped us or looked after us." He was saying something similar to what I was thinking just a minute before.

Miguel reached over and he touched my heart then.

"God can't forget about you. He is with you all the time."

There was a boom then, and a loud one. Then another and another. It scared us good, and we both set up on our little raft.

"What was that?" I asked Miguel. But he didn't get a chance to answer. *Pop, pop, pop!* All of a sudden there was explosives up in the sky, and afore you knowed it, there was blue and red and yellow lights everywhere.

"Fireworks!" Miguel says. *"¡Cohetes!"*

We watched 'em for a while. It was an awful bully sight. They was coming from the other side of the mountain, but it felt like they was shooting right up over our raft and meant jus' for us.

"The baseball game is over," Miguel says.

"They won?"

"Si, *muchacho*. They won." His face was changing colors all the time, on account of the explosives. But I seen him smile.

CHAPTER 26

What Made the Ghost Cry

THEN we passed under all such bully bridges as they have in Los Angeles and right by all them skyscratchers too. We was finally right up under 'em, and it remembered me of a couple nights ago when I first seen 'em from far away. In Los Angeles, generally they sprinkle their skyscratchers around all over, which is different than most cities do. But there's one place in the middle where there's a whole bunch of 'em together, and that's the part that looks like a proper city. It was monstrous beautiful that night with the stars a-twinkling above us and the citylamps a-twinkling under them and the river a-curving right through it all.

It's lovely to be on a raft. We had the sky up there, all speckled with stars, and we laid on our backs and looked up at them some more after the explosives had gone away.

"I reckon we'll be there by morning," I says to Miguel after a time. "We'll find Tom, and he'll take us to his Aunt Polly. She'll know what to do." Miguel he didn't say nuthin back but just kept staring up at the stars.

"I'll bet she can make you legal and proper, so as you can stay with your family."

"It won't work, Huck." That's all he said at first, and immediously I knowed he was feeling lowdown about his situation.

"But—"

"There's no way. I'm just a poor Mexican, and nobody's going to help me. You should go find your friend, and I will keep going on the river. All the way to the ocean."

I couldn't believe he was saying it now, after all we been through together.

"Maybe I'll float all the way down to San Diego. I can hide there a few months. Then maybe I can see my family again, if things get better here."

"I'll come with you!" I says to him, and I meant it when I said it. "We can have a whole nuther 'venture. Out on the ocean!" And now my brain really got going. "There'll be sharks and whales. Prob'ly even some pirates. We'll join up with 'em, and we'll find a treasure on a deserted island!" I was painting a picture with my 'magination. You prob'ly think I was on the wrong track, but I figgered maybe I could get Miguel to think about how he'd need me if he went a-floating out onto the deep ocean. But it didn't work on Miguel.

"It's not safe for you, *muchacho*. I've taken you too far already. You need to get off this raft and back to a regular boy's life."

"If you're a-keeping going, then I'm a-keeping going." I meant it too. He didn't say nuthin for a long while. And when he did say something it was most like a whisper.

"Okay, you win Huck." I was happy then, but I shoulda knowed better than to trust him at a time like that.

We was silent some more for a whiles, and then I fell asleep and dreamed about whales and squids and pirates. But they warn't the bully kind of dreams that makes you feel good inside, but the darker kind of dreams where a body's scared of every little thing that he sees or hears. It was on account of Miguel saying that he wanted to leave me behind and go on hisself all alone.

I didn't stay asleep all night. No, I waked up soon enough, and you'll see that I had a good reason to. I opened my eyes, and I was full awake right away, not like normal when it takes some time. I seen her right away. It was a woman on the shore. When I set up to get a better look, I seen that she was dressed all in white, and she had one of them fabrics hanging over her head, so as you couldn't see nuthin but the shadow of her face. And you're right if you think that maybe it was the same woman I seen our first night on the river. It was most like she was following us on our journey. Well, right away I knowed she was either a ghost or a witch, or at least I suspicioned so. She was a-weeping too—just like the first time I seen her—and she seemed to be looking for someone or something that she'd lost.

"La Llorona." It was Miguel, and he whispered it to me. I looked back at him and he seen her too, and his eyes was all big, like he knowed true well that she was a ghost or a witch. He knowed somehow who she was, and he told me in his whisper voice.

"She is the crying lady. Where I come from, they tell of a woman who fell in love with a man who would not have her. She killed her children in hopes that he would fall in love with her. But still he would not love her. And so she killed herself too. *Se mato.*"

"She's really a ghost?" I had to ask it, 'cause he hadn't said it straight.

"She wanders the earth forever, looking for her lost children. She will never stop crying."

She was in the shadows now, and I couldn't barely

make her out now, but as we passed, I swear she turned and looked me straight in my eyeballs. I was so afeard, I couldn't look away from her.

"*Mis hijos*—" And she seemed to say it to me, like she thought I was one of her children that she'd killed. And then she screamed. "*¡Mis hijos!*" It was the most dreadful thing you ever heard. I wished right then that I'd never heard it and neither looked at her straight in the eyes. But I can't never forget it no matter how hard I try. I wanted to tell her that it warn't me and that she'd have to keep a-looking for her dead children somewheres else. But it warn't easy to find your voice to conversate with a ghost.

We kept on drifting past her, but she kept on a-wailing. "*¡Donde están mis hijos!*"

You can be thankful that you warn't there to see Llorona and are only jus' hearing me tell about it.

We Leave the River
Behind Us

WE hadn't seen Pap since before we got taken in by the Movement people, and there warn't no sign of him now. But I seen Miguel looking hither and forth acrosst the river, and I knowed he was keeping the lookout for Pap or even the 'thorities. But it was peaceable then, and there warn't nobody to bother us after the ghost. There was a place where somebody had drawed all kind of pictures on the side of the river, most like she was making a painting on the concrete. Some was even bully pictures like a wild Injun would make.

And right near there was a whole bunch of ducks—there must've been over a thousand—and they was all sleeping with one eye open and one eye closed. Miguel he said that they would sleep that way so that half their brain was still awake and a-looking out for something that would want to eat them, like a coyote. I thought we might could try it some time, on account we needed half our brain to stay awake and watch out for Pap to come back.

There was trains running on one side of the river now. For a while we went right alongside a train that was moving south just like we was, and it most felt like we warn't alone in our journey no more. But after a while the train cut over the river on a little bridge and went off in the eastern direction, and I wondered if maybe it was headed to Missouri. So we was alone again.

I steered us over to the side of the river, on account I had to uricate real bad and it didn't seem right to take a leaker right in the river that had done so much good for us. I clumb up the concrete and went right up to where the fence was. On the other side was a parking lot full of trucks, and most of 'em had been smashed up in accidents. At another time I might have wanted to go up over that fence and 'splore 'round those trucks for a bit, but I knowed that we had to keep going to find my friend Tom Sawyer, and that this warn't the time for that kind of 'venture.

When I come back down to the raft, I seen Miguel on his knees like he was a-praying again, but this time on his own. I heard him saying something in Mexigrant but I couldn't make it out. He stopped when he heard me come close, and I didn't say nuthin to him about it.

We got back on our raft and kept on going. The river got monstrous wide now, and it didn't feel like a river no more but more like a freeway with no cars and a stripe of water down the middle. It made the raft feel even smaller than it done before. If any person had been looking down there from up above, it woulda been easy to spot us. But there warn't nobody out, 'cause they was all sleeping in their beds on account there was nobody chasing 'em.

I was always one for a 'venture, and all sort of bully things had happened to me and Miguel since we went on the lam. But right then it was dreadful lonesome, and I felt some bit of jealosity for the people who was sleeping with their families. They warn't far from us at all in one way, but they was near on a thousand mile from us in the other way. Miguel he was feeling the same thing, though he didn't say it. Or at least it felt that way to me. We even heard a horse a-braying somewheres back there. You wouldn'ta thunk they'd have a horse right in the middle of the city like that, but sometimes they do. It remembered me and Miguel of the stables, and we was even more quiet now on account of the memberance.

Time was real slow that night, but 'ventually there started to be a glow of light on the horizontal. It was the sun coming up, just as you guessed. Pretty soon we seen a splinter of light, and pretty soon after that the sun was full up, but still hanging low like he warn't yet sure he wanted to go all the way. There was some way that this day seemed different than all the rest of our days on the river. Seemed like maybe this day was a-gonna bring change to me and Miguel. Or maybe I'm just saying that now, 'cause I know what happened later and what change come. Some time it's hard to remember what you was thinking at a earlier time, because it's gotten all mixed up in your brain with what come next.

There was a whole bunch of birds resting in the river, but they got scared off by our little raft. They made a big kermotion when they went off into the sky, and Miguel said they was seabirds, and it was proof that we was coming closer to the ocean. And then we passed a group of turkeys that was resting on the river. You think I'm lying but I ain't. They was prob'ly pet turkeys who had escaped and not the wild ones. But they was still turkeys.

Well not too long after them turkeys I seen the bridge. It was the same bridge that Tom Sawyer had taken me to on my first day in Los Angeles. So I called out to Miguel that we was finally here. Just as we come under the bridge, I immediously jumped out and pulled the raft out of the water and up on the concrete.

"We made it!" I smiled when I said it too, on account I was trying to help Miguel stay hopeful about his situation. I was already thinking about what Tom Sawyer would say when he seen me again and not alone but with an illegal Mexigrant who was on the run from the 'thorities. I hoped maybe his aunt was close by and that she'd know how to help Miguel. But Miguel was full of seriosity.

"There's something I want to tell you, Huck."

"We're almost there!" I says to him. "C'mon, help me with the raft."

We made up our brains to hide the raft in case we might need to come back for it. We tucked it up in the dark place under the bridge where nobody would think to look for a fugitive watercraft. I was ready to go look for Tom then, but Miguel he stopped me.

"Listen to me, Huck. I want to tell you the story of how I came to be here." So I listened, and Miguel told me about how he come to Los Angeles from Mexico and what happened to his pap.

"When we came to America, it was a very hard journey. First there was a train, and it was very dangerous. But then we had to travel very far on foot. Through the *desierto*, the desert. It was very, very hard. Even for me, and I was a boy, young and healthy."

It was a strange time to tell a sad story such as that, but I seen that Miguel wanted to tell it real bad, so I listened to him.

"My father, he was older." Miguel catched hisself now, most like he wanted to cry but was trying hard not to do it. "He did not make it." And now I seen why he was so serious.

"He protected me, *muchacho*," Miguel says. "He carried me. He gave me his water, so that I could drink. He wanted me to have a better life."

I seen now what he was doing. He was trying to make me feel the seriosity of the situation. But I was inclined to be more hopeful about it.

"Don't worry," says I. "We're gonna make it. I promise." I didn't know for sure whether to believe it myself, but it's what I wanted him to think.

CHAPTER 28

Me and Tom Sawyer
Are Reunified

I remembered pretty good how to get to Tom's school. We went to the front and stood acrossed the street where there was some cars to hide behind. We had to wait a bit before school started, but pretty soon there was cars and buses and other such vehiculars as brung the teachers and students to school every day. We kept a close lookout for Tom, but he warn't there. And I started thinking that maybe he'd taken the day off to do bully pirate stuff, but I hoped it warn't so, 'cause we'd have a considerable difficult time finding him in the city, if he warn't here.

But then one of the very last school buses drove up, and Tom Sawyer come out of it with all kind of other kids crowded 'round him. Well he was laughing and yelling, just like you'd think Tom Sawyer would do, and it gave me a warm feeling to see him again after such a long time away. I had used my blade to pop off the mirror of a car, and I used it to misdirect the sun rays over toward him. I seen it afore in a TV show how you could use a mirror as a way to signal somebody whose tension you wanted.

He was just about to go into the school building, when I seen him blinker a couple time. I must've got him in the eye, and he looked over acrossed the street, and I made to wave. He seen me then, but there was a teacher there so he couldn't jus' run over and say hullo. We watched him go inside the school, and Miguel he was suspeptical that Tom would come back out.

"Just holt on, Miguel," says I to him. "You don't know Tom Sawyer like I do. He'll find a way to get hisself free."

So we waited a bit, and sure enough, before you knowed it, we seen a hand come out of one of the windows on the first floor. After that the rest of Tom Sawyer come out, slithering through the tiny little opening just like a snake would. He told us later how he had to tell a bully lie to his teacher so as she'd let him go to the bathroom first thing before school even started. And then he'd clumb up on a garbage can to get through the window, which was way up high to prevent every kid in the school from 'scaping all the time.

After he got hisself out the window, Tom Sawyer dropped right to the ground and run acrossed the street to us. Me and Miguel had taken up a hiding place around the corner in an alley where there was a dumpster big enough to hide a grown Mexigrant and a boy from St. Petersburg. Tom Sawyer didn't have no trouble finding us on account he has a nose for hiding places like that. Well I just about burst to see him, after all that had happened since the trial. And he was happy to see me too. He knowed all about what had happened at the house, on account it was in all the papers, and he said that everybody was on the lookout for Miguel.

I told him straight out that Miguel warn't to blame and that it was my Pap. And Tom Sawyer believed me 'cause he was my true friend. He shook Miguel's hand then on account he didn't have no reason to be afeard of him. And his 'pinion of Miguel only increased when I told how Miguel saved my life and how me and him had 'scaped down the river on a raft we made of junk. The first thing I asked him was about Ms. Douglas and Miss Watson. He said that they warn't dead but they was hurt real bad and was prob'ly still in the hospital. Well it made us feel a little bit better to know that Pap hadn't killed 'em, but it warn't enough to make me and Miguel feel full better.

Tom was monstrous proud of his Aunt Polly, so he was convicted that she would help us and get Miguel free. "She sure is the smartest person I ever met," says he, and I remembered that it warn't the first time he told me so. So we all left our hiding place behind the dumpster—we did a doublecheck for spies first—and we started a-walking, with Tom Sawyer leading the way to where his Aunt Polly had her office. I told Tom to choose the smaller streets where there warn't likely to be policecops who would notice us and try to arrest Miguel. And on the way I told him all about all the stuff that had happened to us along the river and all the people we'd met and all the critters who had visited us.

I told him how Miguel most killed Pap 'stead of Pap killing me and how I found the big pipe that went down to the river and most drowned us. Miguel told how we found the stuff to make the raft and how we done it together to make it seaworthy. But he left it to me to tell the good part where Pap was shooting at us from the bridge up high and we managed to 'scape without any bullet holes through us.

Then there was the Colonel who cooked us up some fish he caught from the river, and Tom's eyes was so big they most bulged out of his face. "They got fish in the river? Our river? Really? Was they good?" he asked us. And we told him how good and tasty they was, especially when you ain't eaten in a good while. "That's so dope," he said, on account I hadn't yet convicted him to do it proper and call something bully that was bully. I tried to tell Tom Sawyer about the Colonel's speechifying, but Tom got bored pretty quick and asked me to keep a-going with the more 'venturous parts of the story.

He got interested again when I told him 'bout the snake that bit Miguel and how I had to hocus a rapscallion to get the medicine that saved Miguel's life. "How big was it?" and Miguel guessed that the snake was 'bout the length of his arm, but I guessed it was two or three times that big. Then Tom Sawyer wanted to know what happened to it and whether we thought a rattlesnake could swim or not. I told him that warn't the point and that the most important part was that Miguel most died but didn't. Well he said he was sorry then, but Miguel didn't get sore about it. Tom Sawyer thought it was a bully trick I played on the Duke, but of course he called it dope instead. Tom thought maybe the Duke had gotten stuck up on that fence for good and maybe starved up there, and all that was left was his skeleton bones. It was a monstrous gruesome thought, and a bully one too, but I didn't think that the Duke was such a bad fellow that you'd want to see him starve and rot away on a fence. He was a-gonna help me before he found out I was famous. That's what I told Tom, and so he adjusticated his hopes so that the Duke 'ventually got down with the help of the crooked doctor.

Well here's where I tried to pollergize to Tom Sawyer, on account I come to the part 'bout the Movement. And Tom was confuzzled, 'cause he didn't understand what I was pollergizing for, so I had to 'splain how my great granddad was mean and lowdown to his great granddad. But the pollergy didn't stick, on account Tom wouldn't take it. He said he reckoned that it warn't my fault if I had mean and lowdown folks in my ancestry. He was pretty sure that some of his ancestry was pretty mean and lowdown too, so we was equal on that account. There warn't no way to know for sure, and maybe the best we could hope for was that they was both mean and lowdown and maybe in cahoots all together and done robberies and piracy and all sorts of mischief as a gang.

Then I even told him what Worker Brian said about being careful what I said to him all the time, but he agreed with me that it warn't no way to be a true friend to a person. Well, that just shows you what kind of boy Tom Sawyer was. And he was a good friend of mine too. So we agreed not to be careful at all and instead be true and honest all the time. We even got Miguel to make a pledge to it.

He was most fascernated by our tale of the Flock and MaryAnn, and he said he was sure it was a cult we got mixed up with, until we told him about how they prayed for us and how the Sister had taken our side of it and had let us go on our way. He allowed then that they prob'ly warn't a cult but only a strange kind of church, and he even allowed that he wanted to meet 'em sometime. That was on account of MaryAnn, who I told him 'bout. And he was bully on her too and said that he would marry if I didn't first. But of course he was a good friend and said I had a priority claim since I met her first and had already breaked bread with her.

I had forgotten to tell about the trap that Pap set for us, so I told it to Tom Sawyer here, and he said it was true that Pap was clever. There warn't telling what he would do to get me and Miguel and kill us dead. And Tom Sawyer said he figgered Pap would want to kill him too on account he helped me bust up the drug deal and was now helping me get lawyer help for Miguel. But he was alright with it and said that he was a-going all the way with us, wherever that would be. He said that me and him was like brothers, and that me and Miguel was like brothers, so that made him and Miguel brothers of a kind, even though they'd just met one and t'other.

Miguel was pleased that we had found Tom, I could tell. "Tom is your family, *muchacho*," Miguel says to me. "Not Pap." And I could tell he meant it too. He said we all had the right to choose our own families and could let go of one to go find another, if we wanted. It was 'specially true, he said, when your first family gave up on you or tried to shoot you, like Pap had done. Then we could start over and not feel bad 'bout it at all. So he agreed that Tom Sawyer and me and even him was all brothers now, so we warn't all alone. I could tell Miguel was thinking on his own family then, and it put a weight on him.

I tells Tom, "Miguel's got a wife already. And a little girl."

"Oh yeah?" says Tom.

"Yeah," says I. "His wife's just about the prettiest Mexigrant you ever seen. And his daughter too."

"I believe it. I sure do," says Tom back. He seen I was trying to cheer up Miguel in a way, and he wanted to help. "What are they called?" Tom Sawyer asked him, and I wondered why I hadn't asked it myself afore this.

Miguel smiled at Tom and said they was called Isabel—that was his wife—and Luna—that was his daughter.

"They live in Arizona," I tells Tom. "But they're coming to be with Miguel as soon as they can." It made Miguel happy to hear me say it, I could tell. And Tom Sawyer said he hoped it would happen real quick.

"Don't worry, Miguel," says Tom. "My Aunt Polly's gonna help us. They sure can't send you back to Mexico after you saved Huck's life." It sounded good, and he sounded full sure about it, but I seen Miguel look down jus' then, and I could tell he didn't full believe it, no matter what he said.

CHAPTER 29

A Surprise
at Aunt Polly's

WE was creeping down an alleyway now, 'cause that's
where Tom Sawyer was a-leading us. At the end of the
alley he said to stop, so we did. He went 'round the corner
to make sure there was no policecops in the proxicality.
After just a few minutes he come back and told us it was
clear as the coast. So we come out of the alley and went
back on to the street, which was bigger here than it was
when we started. Tom brung us to a little building on the
corner that had two levels, and there was a couple small
shops there, like one where you could buy beer and another one where you could wash all the dirt off your dog,
though most dogs I knowed preferred to keep the dirt on
'em. Tom took us up the steps to the second level, 'cause
that's where his aunt worked. I was a little disajointed on
account I was hoping that she worked in a fancy office at
the top of one of them skyscratchers. But Tom Sawyer said
this was where all the smartest lawyers worked.

Tom led us over to a door that said Sawyer and Asso-
ciates written on it, but some of the paint was scratched

off, 'cause somebody had tried to make it say something else. Tom pushed on the door, but it didn't budge for him.

"That's funny," he says. "She's usually here first thing in the morning." So he knocked on the glass real hard, so she would hear him. "Aunt Polly! Aunt Polly!" he says. "It's me, Tom. We got an emergency." It didn't take long for her to show up then. The door opened up just a crack, and she stuck her head out to see what the kermotion was about.

"This is our friend Miguel," says Tom Sawyer, and he points to Miguel when he says it. Well she seen us two then, and she let out a little breath out of her mouth, or maybe she was taking breath in. You see, she was surprised to see us there. "He's got some troubles with the law," Tom tells her. "He sure needs your help."

Miguel he stepped up then, past Tom Sawyer, so as he could talk straight to Aunt Polly and not have Tom as a meddleman. "Don't be afraid. I'm not going to hurt you. And I *don't* want your help." He looked back at me then for just a second and traded eyes with me before he turned back to Aunt Polly. It was like he was sorry to do what he was a-gonna do.

"I've been traveling with this boy. I need to leave him with you. I can't take him with me anymore."

Well it catched me surprised. I guess you could say I shoulda seen it coming the way he'd been talking, but I didn't see it. And it warn't what I wanted to hear.

"No!" I yelled and I grabbed him from behind. But he wouldn't neither even turn 'round to look at me.

"If you have to turn me in, then okay," he tells her, and I couldn't believe what words he was saying. What good was our escape if he just ended up arrested at the end of it? I was yelling at him then, but he didn't pay no tension. "Please. Just take the child and don't let any harm come to him. He's a good boy, and he's helped me a lot. Even saved my life."

Miguel thought he was doing me a good turn, but that's not how I felt about it. It felt mean and lowdown to be double-hocused by a friend like that, and I didn't want to be left behind while Miguel went on the run by hisself. It'd be dreadful lonesome for him without his wife and daughter and even without me.

I told him so then. I told him that I was a-coming with him and that I warn't gonna stay with Tom Sawyer and his Aunt Polly and that he needed me and even that I needed him too. But he wouldn't look down at me. He knowed that he couldn't do it if he looked me straight in the eyes, 'cause it warn't the right thing to do.

"Please," he told Aunt Polly. And the door finally opened the whole way. For a second, we all thought that Miguel had won her over and that I was all set to be left behind. But it was worse even than that.

It was Pap. When the door swung open, he was there, standing right behind Aunt Polly with a gun. And he pointed it straight at Miguel.

"You ain't goin' nowheres," he says to Miguel. "And neither is that no-good son a' mine." He looked straight at me then, and I seen that the rabies was full strong in him. "You hear that you slimy little—"

But he didn't get a chance to finish, on account of Miguel yelling at me to run. And even more, he did something more brave than I ever seen before. He rushed at Pap fast, even though Pap had the gun and Miguel didn't have no weapon of any kind. He got his hands on the gun and pushed it up, so Pap couldn't aim it at him no more. And Miguel was so strong he pushed Pap right back into Aunt Polly's office, and Aunt Polly got pulled back in there with 'em. And the door slammed shut, so me and Tom Sawyer was on the outside and the three of them was on the inside. And we didn't have no view to see what was happening or who was winning.

We ducked down behind a garbage can and tried to figger out what to do. There was all sort of fighting noises coming from inside the office, and it was considerable difficult to be stuck outside with no way to help Miguel or Aunt Polly. It was two 'gainst one, but Pap had the gun, and plus he had the rabies that made him more like a wild animal than a man. It was a close match, I thought, and I didn't want to see what would happen if Pap won out.

CRACK! It was a gunshot for sure, and Tom Sawyer and me we didn't say nuthin but traded eyes, 'cause we knowed it was the sign that somebody'd gotten the higher hand in the fight. It was quiet after that, and me and Tom waited, but finally I couldn't wait no more.

"Miguel?" I asked, but not too loud. "You okay?"

There warn't no answer, and it made me afeard that he'd been shot or hurt in some other way. But we did hear some noises in there, like somebody moving 'round, before we heard a voice through the glass door.

"That's the kind of son you are." It was Pap and not Miguel. "More worried about an illegal Mexigrant than your own father."

Well I was desperated now. "What did you do to him?" I yelled. And thanksfully Miguel answered right back telling me he was okay. But you could tell he warn't in a strong position with Pap.

"He's okay for now," says Pap. "But I still got a gun pointed straight at his dirty Mexigrant face."

"Run boys!" It was Aunt Polly's voice now. "Get the police!"

I looked back at Tom Sawyer and we traded eyes again.

"Now I wouldn't do that," says Pap. "When the police get here, they're gonna find one dead grasshopper, and one dead lady too. You boys understand that, don't ya?"

"What do you want?" says I.

"Gimme a minute. I'm thinkin'."

So we waited for Pap to tell us what he wanted. That's when I seen an aeroplane in the sky, flying right over us. It was coming down too, so as it could land at the airport there in Los Angeles. I don't know why I remember that aeroplane so well, but I do.

"I want a ticket on that raft," Pap says. "You boys discovered the best escape route in town. And it's only a matter of time before them coppers catch up with me."

Well my brain started turning it over. It seemed like maybe Pap thought that the policecops already knowed that it was *him* that hurt Ms. Douglas and Miss Watson, and not Miguel. It warn't a fond thought to think of Pap on the raft, either with me or without me. But running for the policecops warn't a good option neither at that point. I couldn't see clear how it would all work out.

So I asked him, "What about Miguel?"

"I reckon he don't have to get hurt, if you boys help me get away free and clear."

And Tom spoke up too. "What about Aunt Polly?"

"Her neither, I suppose. Whaddya say boys? We got a deal?"

Aunt Polly screamed out then, trying to get us to go to the policecops, but Pap told her to shut up and must've waved the gun around too, 'cause after that she didn't make no more noise.

Me and Tom Sawyer traded eyes again. I knowed he was thinking the same thing as me. This was like a bargain with Beelzebub, as they say, and could end up getting all of us dead. But there warn't nobody else there to bargain with *but* Beelzebub.

CHAPTER 30

We Go from Fugitives to Hostagers

SO we went inside. It was a little office, and in the front part, the place where people waited to see Aunt Polly, there was jus' a desk and a couple of plastic chairs. Miguel was on the floor, and Pap had the gun pointed straight at him. He knew he didn't have to point the gun at us as long as he had it pointed at our friend. We warn't in no position to try to turn the situation around. Aunt Polly was stand-

ing over with her back 'gainst the wall. She warn't crying or nuthin and instead was acting strong and courageful, jus' like you'd expect from one of Tom Sawyer's relations.

It was the first time I got a good look at my Pap since that horrible night at Ms. Douglas's home. I didn't think it would be possible, but he looked even worse off now than he did back then. His hair was wild, and his eyes was like glass. He had a limp too and seemed to be dragging his left foot, and I suspicioned that he'd hurt hisself when he fell over the railing and down to the first level of Ms. Douglas's house. Seeing how he was in pain jus' to walk, I wondered at how he had kept up with us on the river after he'd set the shopping car trap for me and Miguel. I knowed that it warn't gonna be easy to get free of him now, seeing as how he was so close to winning his war against us and going free with the help of our raft. There was a flask of whiskey on the desk, and I knowed that Pap had brung it, not Aunt Polly.

"Well, lookee here," he says when he seen us come through the door. "The heroes is back together again. First they done taken what was rightfully mine and put me on the wrong side of the law. And now here they is helpin' an illegal Mexigrant."

We didn't say nuthin back. There warn't nuthin to say to a man like that even if you was his son. I wished I'd discovered it a long time earlier. It warn't clear to me whether he purposed to take us along on the raft or leave us behind or even go back on his word and kill all of us dead. He warn't one that could easily be predicated like that, even by a body who was related by blood.

"Set down over there a whiles," and he pointed over at the plastic chairs that was meant for people to wait in. He took a swig from his flask now and then set down in the chair that was behind the desk. He kept the gun a-pointed at Miguel, but he looked me straight at the eyes.

"Ain't I been a father to you? Ain't I tried to learn you how to be a man?"

I didn't know how to 'spond to that. But I figgered out that he meant to stay there a while and have a kind of a father to son talk, 'stead of leaving for the raft right away. I decided to answer him, on account that he was the one with the gun and all of us needed to let the situation play out and maybe look for our chance to turn it 'round.

"You learned me good enough." I tried to say something that agreed with him a bit but was still non-committed, so I would have some room to maneuverate with my words.

"You got no good reason to betray me."

"No sir, I don't." I warn't keen to call him "sir," but you see how the situation called me to do it.

"Well, then why you done it?"

"I ain't done it."

"Don't give me none o' your lip! I *know* you done it." I'd gotten him stirred up again, so now he got up and waved the gun at my face, and I had to turn my head up to look into his glass eyes. "Didn't I bring you here so as we could have a better life? Didn't I? That's what a father does for a son."

I didn't say nuthin, 'cause I didn't want to jus' then.

"You and me was gonna be rich. I was gonna clean up

and be a better father to you. Didn't I tell you that?" He was softening up in a way, and I suppose I coulda played it nice and easy and tried to get him to calm down, but I didn't. There was a part of me that didn't even care that he had that gun right in my face.

"It ain't true," I says, and I said it right at his eyes.

"What'd you say?"

"I said it ain't true. It warn't never gonna happen the way you said."

"Listen to you. You're callin' me a liar? What would your mama say to hear you say a thing like that to your Pap?"

Well he shouldn'ta brung her into it. It warn't right to do it, and I wanted him to know it. "She ain't here to say nuthin," I says. "She ain't here 'cause you killed her dead, didn't you?"

I never said it before. I warn't even a thousand percent sure that it was true. But still I was pretty sure. It was an ugly thought, and most times I tried not to think on it. But here it come out at the wrongest time you could ever 'magine.

He hit me then. With the gun. I didn't neither feel it at first, but then the pain come and come hard. Aunt Polly screamed, and Miguel he jumped up to come to my help. But Pap was quick and right away had the gun pointed straight at Miguel's head.

"Do not hurt him again," says Miguel. "Or I will—"

"Or you'll what?" says Pap, knowing that he's got a gun and Miguel don't.

"He's a good boy," says Miguel.

POP! Pap fired the gun. It didn't hit no one, but it scared us all pretty good. It made a hole in the wall behind Miguel.

"Shut up!" yells Pap at Miguel. "You dirty Mexigrant. What do you know about my boy?" Well Miguel backed down then. He didn't have no good choice.

By this time there was blood coming out of my nose, and I used my shirt to hold it in.

"It's true, ain't it?" I says to him, and the pain made me say it loud and hard. "You killed her." For some reason, I warn't ready to end the conversating without which he told me the truth about my mama.

"That lyin' bitch deserved it." He said it right to my eyes. Well it most breaked my heart to hear it. I already knowed it was true, but it was different hearing him say it aloud and even saying that it was her fault.

"Don't talk about her like that." I said it strong as I could, despite I had tears coming out of my eyes. But it worked. Pap got quiet after that and set back down. We was all quiet then. Pap looked like he'd had the tuck all taken out of him. I most felt sorry for him then, 'cause I knowed he was sick with the rabies and maybe it was just the rabies that had made him do it. Maybe the rabies was 'sponsible for all of it. Maybe he was all rabies now, and not even my Pap no more. Maybe it had been that way for a long while.

CHAPTER 31

A Showdown
on the River

AFTER a while, Pap got some of his gumpshun back. He dug around in the desk and come out with some goose tape. He told me to tape Aunt Polly to her chair, so as she wouldn't be able to call the policecops right when we left. I was relieved to do it on account it meant that he didn't mean to kill her.

"Make it nice and tight," he tells me. "I don't want her makin' no phone calls or sendin' no faxes or nuthin like that." Well, I done it even though my heart warn't in it. I whispered in her ear as I was doing it, so as she would know.

"I'm awful sorry, Aunt Polly."

Pap was trying to muster up some optimystical ideas now. "Maybe we'll float all the way down to San Diego. Maybe even go acrossed into his country illegal. See how he likes that!" He raised his flask and smiled at Miguel, most like he was making fun of him. "We'll be bandidos!"

He swiveled 'round on his chair so as he could have a view outside. "It's a beautiful day for a boat ride, huh?"

Aunt Polly seen him do it, and she leaned in real close to me then, so she could whisper in my ear. "You can't go with him," she tells me. "Huck, he will kill you. You have to get away. You understand?"

"Hey what's she sayin', son?" Pap had swiveled back 'round, but he hadn't heard it clear. "I don't want no more talk outta her. If I don't hear nuther word of bitchin' from a nuther woman the whole rest of my life, that'll still be too soon for me."

He got up now and grabbed some papers from the desk. He crumbled 'em up good and then stuck 'em in her mouth, and he warn't gentle about it. Then he took some of the tape and put it over her mouth. It hurt me to see it too, 'cause I seen that it warn't comfortable for Aunt Polly. Tom Sawyer jumped up too, making to defend his aunt, but Miguel held him back, so he wouldn't get into it with Pap. I seen she was okay and could still breathe alright through the holes in her nose. That was one good thing. After that Pap had me tie up Miguel's hands behind his back, so as he couldn't fight or do nuthin else.

"Alright," Pap says. "Let's get down to the river before it gets any later."

Miguel made one last try to leave me behind, and Tom Sawyer too. But Pap warn't inclined to go with just one hostager. "Those coppers don't care if I shoot you," he says to Miguel. "But they sure care about these boys. They make for better protection." So I tried to convict him to let Miguel stay behind like Aunt Polly. But Pap's blood had gone bad for Miguel, and I seen right away that the only two options available was Miguel coming with us as a hostager or leaving him behind as a dead body.

Pap had me and Tom Sawyer go first out the door, then Miguel, then Pap come behind in the very back. He was holding his gun in his jacket pocket now, so it warn't obvious that we was under gunpoint. He used Aunt Polly's keys to lock the door behind him, and I traded eyes with her once more before the door shut. She was trying to tell me to be brave with her eyes, and my eyes heard it too, loud and clearly.

When we come down the steps, Pap had us wait and he had a quick look 'round. He was afeard that there might be policecops around but he didn't see none, so he had us go out on the street. But immediously we went 'round the back to the smaller street, like the one Tom had us come in on. I was thinking how things had changed so much in just a short while. On the way in, I was afeard of seeing any policecops, and now I was hoping that we might run into one or two or even more.

"Now don't try nuthin, you little toads," Pap says like he was reading my brain. "Or your compadre here is gonna pay for it."

It was a long walk, prob'ly 'cause Tom Sawyer was leading us and trying to go slow and give us more time to get out of the mess we was in. And all the time I was turning over different ideas in my brain. Maybe I could make a run for it. But then Pap might shoot Miguel or Tom Sawyer or even me. Maybe I could make a signal to somebody. But there warn't nobody to signal. And how would I signal 'em anyway? There warn't no way to make sure they'd get the right idea and find a way to help us that wouldn't get us all killed, and them killed too maybe.

I had my eyes wide open, looking hither and forth for some way out, but trying not to let Pap in on it. It was still early in the morning, so there warn't a lot of folk out yet. A couple cars drove by, but they didn't pay us no tension on account we just looked like a couple of boys and a couple of men out for a walk, without which they could see Miguel's hands tied behind his back with tape. I seen one policecop on a motorcycle, but he was going crossways to us on a different street, and I don't neither think he seen nuthin, and prob'ly wouldn'ta stopped even if he had.

Tom led us straight to the bridge, and it was strange to think that we'd come there that first day we met afore we was even friends. He squeezed through the fence, and I followed him, just like we done that day when we was hunting crawfish. Miguel come next. You might think I'da had a plan to get Pap stuck on the fence, just like I done with the Duke, but there warn't a good place to do it here, and plus Pap had a gun, which the Duke didn't.

All four of us scrambled down the slanted concrete, with Pap at the rear. And then Pap told me and Tom Sawyer to go up to the dark place under the bridge to get the raft and bring it down to the water. He and Miguel stayed below, and Pap still had the gun pointed at Miguel. Now that we was off the street and under the bridge I knowed we was in trouble, 'cause we was hidden from view down there, and even if a policecop come by there wouldn't be no chance he would see us. So I knowed we was on our own, and it made me feel like maybe there warn't no hope left. Me and Miguel had most got ourselves killed over and over, and now we was about to get on a raft with a man who was afflected with the rabies and capable of near on anything. And now my friend Tom Sawyer was along too, and he didn't neither deserve to get catched up with a man such as Pap.

Me and Tom traded eyes when we got the raft, and we dragged it down the ramp. It warn't too heavy, so we made quick work of it, and pretty soon the raft was floating in the channel again, and I was using my pole to keep us from floating away. Pap made Tom get on and then Miguel too.

"Well let's get goin'," he says. "That ocean is waitin' for us."

Well me and Tom Sawyer traded eyes one last time right then, and I knowed it was time. I brung my pole up out of the water as quick as I could. Tom he ducked down, and I swung the pole right over his head and toward Pap. I did it with all of my might, and I thunk on my mama just then so I would be strong and brave too. Well I got a stroke of luck then, 'cause Pap was looking down, so he didn't see nuthin coming until it was too late.

"What—?" He only got one word out before my pole catched him square in the jaw. He teeter-toppled for a minute before losing his balance and falling into the water. But I lost grip of my pole and it went flying through the air and clatterlanded on the concrete part of the river, which was too far for me to grab it. I was froze solid as ice for a second, but Tom Sawyer knowed what to do.

"C'mon, Huck!" he yells. "Paddle!" Tom Sawyer pushed us off into the water and away from the shore.

Pap was still a-flailing around in the water, trying to recover hisself. Well we warn't in the fastest part of the river, so me and Tom aimed for that, hoping that it would carry us away from Pap. Miguel he was trying to help with his feet, but his hands was still tied, so couldn't properly paddle. We was making progress and most had the raft going pretty good, but then Pap come up out of the water. He looked big as a kraken or some nuther type of monster. He took a couple steps toward us and then made to lunge for the raft, and he made it. His hands grabbed holt of the raft and wouldn't let go. Miguel was kicking him as hard as he could, but Pap was strong with the rabies and so it didn't matter. He started pulling hisself up onto the raft, and I knowed we was done for.

Then I thunk of it. My blade. It was tucked away in my sock, 'gainst my leg. I grabbed it quick and brung it up high and then down as hard as I could. It went straight into Pap's hand, most like he was a crawfish. And he screeched like a wild bird to feel it. With his other hand, he made to swipe at me, but he missed. With one hand in the air and the other hand hurt, he lost his grip and started sliding off our raft. Miguel gave him one last kick, and he fell into the water again. In the meanwhile, Tom Sawyer was paddling as hard as he could, and he finally got the raft over into the fast part of the current. Afore we knowed it, we was a good distance away from Pap and getting further away every second. We all turned back to see him come out of the water. But he warn't done yet. He pulled out his gun now and started shooting shots at us.

Pop-pop-pop-pop! But he was all wet and injured too, so his aim was wild. And he was a-screaming too, but it warn't even words but jus' blood and fury that we'd gotten away from him.

I went over to Miguel and used the blade to cut the tape on his wrists, so he could be free again. "Thank you, *muchacho*," says Miguel. "That was very brave, what you did."

"What *we* did," I says. "Tom was in on it the whole time."

We turned to look at Tom, who was smiling kind of funny. And he was breathing a little rough.

"I think he got me," says Tom.

That's when we seen the blood.

CHAPTER 32

No More River
to Ride

THERE was a siren, and we saw a policecop speeding back the other way. I suppose somebody musta heard all them gunshots and had called the 'thorities to come check where they come from. Maybe Pap was finally gonna get hisself catched.

Me and Miguel and Tom Sawyer was quiet for a long while after the siren passed. It was real still on the river. There warn't no more wildlife, 'cept a few birds that would go flying before we got to 'em. It shoulda been joyful to finally be rid of my Pap, but we was all afflected with melancholera on account of Tom's being shot. Tom said he was okay, 'cause he was jus' shot in the leg. But he was bleeding bad, and we was leaving a trail of blood in the water. Miguel used his belt to squeeze Tom's leg up tight and try to stop all the blood, but it only worked halfway. Tom Sawyer was trying hard to convict us that his life warn't in no danger, but he was losing his gumpshun all the way.

How slow and still the time did drag along. Miguel got real quiet. And Tom Sawyer stopped talking so much on account he was in considerable pain. So I was just alone in my brain, and I thunk on what had happened and how things might come good for all of us. Maybe Miguel was right that the law warn't on our side and that Aunt Polly warn't in a position to help him get back to his family. Well then we'd have to stay on the lam. I knowed there was islands out in the ocean where we could hide out and let Tom Sawyer heal up. It sounded like a bully 'venture to me, but I knowed it warn't what Miguel wanted—he wanted to go back to be with his wife Isabel and his little girl Luna. Maybe he could be convicted that it was the only good choice for us. I thought prob'ly Tom Sawyer could make it to the island, but I warn't a thousand percent sure of it. It tore me up a little bit, knowing that what was right for one of my friends was wrong for the other, but I couldn't see no other way 'round it, no matter how many times I turned it over in my brain.

Well we floated and floated down the river made of concrete, until it seemed to me like we was most to the end. The air smelled different, kinda salty, jus' like it did when I went to the beach with all them Grangerfords. I was sure we was coming close to the ocean. I told Miguel 'bout the islands and how they would due for a good hideaway for three fugitives like us. But he didn't say nuthin back. He took a nuther look at Tom Sawyer's leg and tried to make the belt tighter until Tom yelled out that it hurt.

The river changed again, and we passed through a part that had big rocks on each side and tall grass too. It was getting wild again, after being jus' concrete for a good many miles. It got wide here and deep too, on account the river water was mixing with the ocean. Then, just like I thought it would, the river opened up and fell straight into the ocean. It warn't all of a sudden, but kind of a graduous change. And it warn't neither the ocean proper but more like a carved out part where there warn't no big waves. But still it was the ocean, I could tell. There was more birds here but ocean birds now, like pelicans. I seen one swoop down and slurp up a fish with its gigantic beak. It felt different here, like we was smaller somehow. And I knowed then that I would miss the river that had been a home to us for so many days. I started a-wondering how far the islands was and how our little raft would do in the waves. I hoped that the sharks and squids and whales would leave us all alone and that we wouldn't get bothered by pirates. We was finally rid of my Pap, and I didn't want no more trouble with people who wanted to hurt us, especially with Tom Sawyer already shot.

I started talking to Tom about the islands and how we'd find a cave where he could rest. When he was better, we'd go 'sploring in the cave and see if we couldn't find some buried treasure. And we'd climb all over the island and see what else we could find and maybe have a battle with some wild Injuns, if they still lived free up in them hills. It was bully by him, he said, but I could tell he warn't in no position to show the proper 'mount of 'thusiasticism. He was real courageful though and told me how bully it would be on the island. And he told Miguel that we'd stay there as long as we needed to before it was safe to go back to his family. Even at a time like that, Tom Sawyer was thinking about Miguel and his predictament and was trying to make him feel better about it.

The ocean started getting wider and wider, and I started to feel better about how things had turned out for us. It
was the end of our journey in one way, or at least the end
of one part of our journey. And we'd made it without neither getting killed or getting Miguel arrested. We was all
still alive and free. And Tom Sawyer was gonna be alright,
I knowed it. I'd even say a prayer for him if it would help.

We passed under a concrete bridge that had cars on
it, but they didn't pay us no tension. And we kept floating
out toward the sun, which was real bright and high that
day. The water was sparkling like diamonds, and it made a
body happy to be in a place like Los Angeles. There warn't
no ocean in St. Petersburg, and the sun warn't so bright
as it was here. And I was also feeling that maybe I'd finally
gotten free of my Pap for good. It warn't sure, but I had
a warm and comfortable feeling like it was so. I started to
paddle with my hands on account the waves were a-coming in. They was small waves, real nice and slow, but still
they had the effect of slowing our little raft down.

Well we was coming up on a little pier that stuck out
into the ocean. It was right afore the ocean opened up real
wide, and there was just a few men on the pier with their
fishing poles. There was a couple Mexigrants and a couple
of other men too. They warn't paying us no tension, but I
seen Miguel keeping a close eye on 'em like he was worried they was the last hurdle atwixt us and the wide ocean.
But they didn't say nuthin and we floated right by. We was
home free, as they say.

But then I seen Miguel stand up. He looked at Tom

Sawyer a minute, then turned back to the men fishing on the pier.

"Help!" he yelled. "Excuse me! Help!" And they all turned to look at us now. "*¡Auxilio! ¡Auxilio!*" He used the Mexigrant word too on account of the Mexigrants up there.

"No!" I yelled at him. But he was already in the water. It made for a big splash, and then he was swimming along with the raft, pushing it back toward the pier.

"This boy needs help!" he yelled up at 'em. "*¡Ayúdenme por favor!*" And I seen a couple of the men start scrambling down the rocks on the side of the pier. He was sacrificializing hisself on account of Tom. And it made me feel mean and lowdown to know it.

CHAPTER 33

The End
of the 'Venture

EVERYTHING happened fast then. Them fishing fellows helped Miguel pull the raft up on the rocks, and then a couple of 'em helped Tom Sawyer out over the rocks and onto the grass where he could lay down. Somebody called the policecops and it warn't just a couple minutes before the first ones got there.

I was hopeful that Miguel could slip away, and maybe even I could go with him. But those fishermen must've knowed who we was, 'cause they made a kind of circle 'round him while they waited for the policecops to come. They warn't mean or angry or nuthin, but they let Miguel know that he warn't in a position to run.

Tom Sawyer was on the ground, breathing fast and still bleeding out through his jeans. But those fellows said that he'd be okay when he got to the hospital. I told him to hang on and that I'd come visit him no matter where he was. When the policecops come, one of 'em went straight to Tom Sawyer and radioed in for an ambulance to come pick him up. The other one stood near to Miguel, and I seen Miguel and him say a couple of words together, but I couldn't hear what. He didn't take Miguel right away, but instead let Miguel kneel down by Tom Sawyer and me.

"You're going to be okay," Miguel says to Tom. "The doctors are on their way."

Well Tom Sawyer said thank you and told Miguel how brave he was and how he was gonna get Aunt Polly to help him, so he could go back to his family. Miguel didn't believe him but pretended that he did, so as Tom wouldn't feel too bad about it.

Then he turned to me. I warn't in the mood to say no goodbyes, but Miguel was.

"We can't run anymore, *muchacho*. You're a man now, *un hombre hecho y derecho*. Tom needs you. Ms. Douglas and Miss Watson need you. You understand?"

Well I didn't understand, but I said goodbye to Miguel anyway. The policecop took him off to the car now and I seen him put fisticuffs on my friend who ain't done nuth-

in but save my life and protect me from my Pap. It warn't how I wanted the story to end, but Miguel had made his choice. That's how it is. If the gov'ment's got it in for you, then it don't matter if you's a good man or not.

They was loading Tom Sawyer into the back of the ambulance when a long black car rode up. I recognified it right away as Judge Thatcher's, and I was right. He come out the back, just like before, and I run up to him right away.

"He didn't do nuthin wrong," I says. I told him all about Miguel and Pap then, how Miguel had saved my life and how Pap had shot Tom Sawyer. I tried to keep the words straight, so he would understand that Miguel couldn't be taken to jail, but they come out all jumbled on account I was trying to say everything all at one time.

"Now calm down, son," he says to me. "We've got plenty of time to sort through what happened."

He went and checked on Tom Sawyer before they closed the back doors of the ambulance. They'd met each other at the trial, so it was a reunification in a way. Tom told him that he was okay, though he was real weak I could tell. Judge Thatcher said that he'd send the policecops to rescue Aunt Polly and she'd meet him at the hospital.

Me and Tom Sawyer traded eyes right before they closed the doors.

"We'll save him, Huck," he says to me. "Don't worry." He was talking about Miguel, but I'd run out of hopes for that.

As the ambulance drove off, I told Judge Thatcher again.

"He didn't do nuthin wrong."

"I know, Huck."

"He saved my life."

"I know."

"It was my Pap."

"They picked your father up, son," Judge Thatcher says. "He's going to jail." It was hard to believe it was true, after everything he'd done and everything he'd put us through. It seemed like maybe I warn't never gonna be free of him. But Judge Thatcher was a truthful man, so I made up my brain to believe him despite my doubtables.

"He can't hurt you anymore," he says. And I hoped he was right.

CHAPTER 34

How It All Come Out in the End

As you know, I ain't never been much for praying. But I reckoned that there was times that called for it, and a body had to make adjustications to the situation sometime. You see, it was Miss Watson that had got the worst of Pap's attack with his knife. Judge Thatcher took me to see her in the hospital. She was laying real still and couldn't talk or move or nuthin. The Judge left me alone with her, and I felt mean and lowdown to think that it was my blood that done it to her.

So's I got down on my knees. That's the proper way to pray, as you know. And I did my best to pray for her and asked God to make her better and said sorry that I brung such a man as Pap into contact with folks that was so regular and decent. I don't know if I done it right, but I figgered that if it was me a-laying in that bed 'stead of Miss Watson, that she'd be a-praying for me, and so it was right for me to try to do the same for her. I was just 'bout to get up, when I felt her hand. It moved a little bit and grabbed mine, which was in the proper praying position

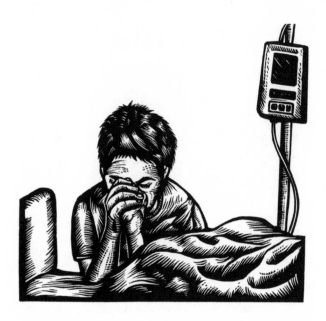

being folded up with the other one. I knowed that she was gonna be alright then, and it made a body feel good. I don't know if the praying had anything to do with it, but I'm glad I done it either way.

As for Ms. Douglas, she was okay after all and not as badly hurt as Miss Watson was, but she still had to ride in a wheely-chair 'cause of what Pap done to her. But the doctor said it was only temporal and she'd be able to go hiking in the woods again as soon as she healed up once and for good. Miss Watson even got to feeling better after a while. When she touched my hand was just the beginning, and before you knowed it she was talking and even laughing.

Tom Sawyer was monstrous proud of his injured leg and said that it was indispicable proof that he'd been on a bully 'venture. He even got to using one of his crutches for a saber and gave me the other one so it would be an even fight. Aunt Polly tried to stop us from fighting, but we started up again when she went to get a coffee break. She warn't too mad but just a little when she found out we'd breaked a pretty vase of flowers that a person had sent to Tom Sawyer so as he'd feel better. Tom said it warn't no big deal and that playing sabers had made him feel better even than getting the flowers had, and it was a kind of a bonus that the whole thing ended up with breaked glass and water everywheres all over the room. After she cleaned it all up, Aunt Polly told me that I was a brave boy and she was glad that I fought with my Pap on the river, even though it got her blood relation shot in the leg. Tom Sawyer said we was gonna have all kinds of dope 'ventures once he was all healed up. I was so happy to hear it that I even told him how dope it was, even though what I really meant was bully.

And Pap—well he got sent away once and for good. Judge Thatcher said he won't never get out of jail, on account of all the trouble he caused and the people he hurt. He said that Ms. Douglas and Miss Watson wanted to 'dopt me for good. I said that it'd be alright with me, as long as they didn't try to sivilize me too much. He said he reckoned that nobody couldn't never sivilize me, no matter how they tried.

I told him he didn't neither have to worry about it, 'cause I was inclined to light out for another 'venture before I let it happen too much. And he said he hoped I wouldn't but would make up my brain to stay with them, at least for a whiles.

CHAPTER THE LAST

Nuthin More
to Write

YOU prob'ly think I'm forgetting something, but I'm not. I just been saving the best part for the very last. We had a little party there in the hospital on account we was all still alive and free of Pap. There was balloons there, and I used my blade to pop 'em one by one. You see, I'd gotten my blade back out of Pap's hand before he started shooting at us. And I was pleased to have it too, 'cause it remembered me on my mama.

Well at the end of the party Judge Thatcher took me out of Miss Watson's room and down the hall to the elevation closet, and he let me push the buttons for the bottom floor where he said there was a surprise for me. We went out the door and out on the street. We was waiting for a little bit, and Judge Thatcher wouldn't even give me a clue 'bout what was coming. Well finally there come a white van that had markings like a policecop car. It come 'round a corner then pulled up right to the sidewalk, where me and the Judge was standing.

A policecop got out of the car and come to shake

Judge Thatcher's hand. And then the Judge gave him a piece of paper that had the officious markings of the gov'ment on it. The policecop looked at it for just a second and smiled. Then he opened up the back of the van. I'll bet you guessed it already, but it was Miguel! My heart most burst to see him again. He smiled real big to see me, and I must've been smiling too even though I don't remember it.

Judge Thatcher knowed it would make me happy, so he had the policecop give me his big ring of keys, so as I could let Miguel go free myself. You see, the Judge he had friends who worked for the gov'ment, and he'd made sure Miguel got recognified for being a hero and saving my life, so he wouldn't get sent away back to Mexico. And Isabel and Luna was on their way from Arizona to come be with him too. I won't tell it now, but there's a whole nuther story about how I met his family. Isabel his wife was just as beautiful as her photogram, maybe even more. And Luna was the type of girl you'd want to have a 'venture with, which happened on down the line somewheres, and Tom Sawyer was there too, but I'll wait to tell about it some nuther time. When Miguel was proper free of the fisticuffs, he gave me a tight squeeze and said how happy he was that I was okay and free of my Pap.

And so that's it. There ain't nuthin more to write about, and I am rotten glad of it, 'cause if I'da knowed what trouble it was to make a book I wouldn'ta tackled it. I guess there's some folks who say that what I done warn't right. I shouldn'ta helped Miguel escape, 'cause he's an illegal Mexigrant and even if he ain't killed or attacked nobody, he's still a-taking somebody's job that's got a right to be here. But I reckon if that kind of thinking had any truth in it then you'd just move out to a shack in the desert where nobody'd have no chance to take your job and you could just be left alone forever and ever until you'd fall down dead. That don't make no sense to me, and neither-ways I don't want to be alone no more.

The End

Acknowledgments

Thank you, first, to Mark Twain. My greatest hope is that this book will encourage readers to revisit *The Adventures of Huckleberry Finn.*

Daniel González has been a joy to collaborate with. His creativity, his skill, and his devotion to his craft are inspiring. Christina Roldán Ortega introduced me to Daniel.

Colleen Dunn Bates at Prospect Park Books—whom I met through Lian Dolan—has been extraordinarily generous with her time and expertise. Amy Inouye at Future Studio is responsible for the beautiful design of the book. My editor David Ulin helped bring out the best in the manuscript.

Many friends read early drafts and provided encouragement and feedback: Christine Sowder, Laura DeRoche, Bob Kundrat, Laurel Hoctor Jones, Jonathan Hennessey, and Jay Hirsch. Mark DeRoche has been a sounding board and a true friend.

Others have supported the film version of this story (which is still in the works): Meta Valentic, Max Borenstein, Adam Waldman, Nathan Morse, Morman Boling Casting, Bob and Carole DeRoche, Dave Raven and Rebecca McSparran, and others who are too numerous to name.

My niece Mercedes Perez contributed the delightful word "confuzzled."

This book is dedicated to Simone, Neve, and a progeny to be named later.

— TIM DEROCHE

The images in this book are linocuts that were created in my studio in Highland Park from March through July 2017. Life is a constantly flowing river that sometimes rages and other times is serene. During the time I was creating these images, one life came to an end, and a new one announced its arrival. I want to dedicate this work to the memory of my grandfather Juan and to my only sister's first daughter, my niece, Isabel. May the river take you on many wonderful adventures, and the memory of those who have traveled before you bring you courage to hold fast when it rages.

— DANIEL GONZÁLEZ